WHEN MY

Ship

COMES IN

A Naughty Nautical Romance

ANNIE CHARME

First Published in 2022 by Chambre Rose Publishing

When My Ship Comes In.

Ebook

Print ISBN 978-1-7399906-2-6

Cover Designed by: Annie Charme

Formatted by: Chambre Rose Publishing

❀ Created with Vellum

This book is written by a British author. Therefore all spellings and grammar are British English.

For Ash

However far the stream flows,
it never forgets its source.

For anyone in need of sun, sea, sand,
and a little romance...

CHAPTER One

ZAC

"Zac. You made it," Josh hollers across the atrium as he bounds over to me in his waiter's uniform.

I stand my suitcase up before he grabs my hand, then two jabs to my ribs with his left hook. His classic greeting always stings a bit, but I never let on.

"I can't believe you're here. What's it been? Almost a year?"

"Hey, bro. Something like that." I pat his arm and smile to hide the wince from the pummelling. "Are you at work?"

Josh rubs a hand on the back of his head, ruffling his short, dark hair. "Yeah, I'm on my way there now. I checked the schedule and you start at five."

"Thanks for helping me get this job. I don't know what I would've done."

He slaps my bicep. "No worries. Don't get canned again. I pulled some strings to get you in here. They heard about what happened on your last ship."

I huff out through my nostrils. "You know I was innocent, right?"

Josh flinches his head back and raises his brow.

I let out a long sigh. "All right, maybe I flirted, but that's all. She was the one that propositioned me."

Josh chuckles. "Dude, only you could accidentally get it on with the captain's wife."

"She wasn't the captain's wife. She was married to the captain's brother. I never touched her. It was all a big misunderstanding."

"If you say so." He shakes his head, still chuckling away to himself.

"It's the truth. The husband said it was me propositioning his wife when I actually turned her down. She was double my age, for fuck's sake."

"You like older women."

"Yeah, because they give good tips, not because I want to jump into bed with them."

"Boy. Yes, you there." A voice says behind me. Josh glances over my shoulder at a rich prick in a suit. He waves his hand between us, showing off his Rolex. "Instead of chatting amongst yourselves, make yourself useful and show my wife and I to our cabin."

Josh tugs the navy fabric of his vest and straightens his name badge. "Sir. I work in the restaurant. I'm not a steward."

"I beg your pardon, boy?"

Josh rolls his eyes and pats my shoulder, then leans in so only I can hear him. "Same shit, different ship, ay bro."

"Yep, some things never change. Don't let them grind you down."

"I'm glad you're here. I'll catch up with you later."

He walks away, leading the snooty couple to their cabin.

I drag my case behind me, taking a drink of my bottled water as I make my way to the elevator. The geometric pattern on the carpet moves like a kaleidoscope, making me dizzy until I'm met with red patent heels. My eyes move up her smooth calves, thick thighs to a full behind underneath a red polka dot dress flowing around her shapely body.

I stop in my tracks, admiring the rear view. She turns around, making her long, blonde curls bounce underneath a large black sun hat with a wide rim. Black shades cover her eyes, and I'm not sure if it's me she's staring at or the map she's holding.

Leisurely removing the sunglasses from her face, she peers at me with eyes bluer than the Pacific Ocean. My breath stalls. Her ruby lips curl upwards into the brightest smile. She's stunning. Classy and sophisticated like a movie star. Marilyn Monroe would struggle to take the spotlight from this woman.

My bottle of water slips from my fingers, crashing to the ground along with my stomach as it plummets to the bottom of the seabed.

She yelps and steps back as the water sprays her legs, covering her shiny shoes.

Moving quickly, I drop my case and slide my arm around her to stop her from tumbling. Locking eyes with me, her breath hitches. Fuck. My hand is on her ass. My hand is on her *ass*. Play it cool, just stay cool.

Once she's steady, I remove my hand and casually run it through my hair, but my chest hammers as if a shark is breaking through my ribs. "I'm so sorry, ma'am." I bend down to collect the bottle and drop to my knees to wipe

3

ANNIE CHARME

the water from her smooth legs like a silky ribbon beneath my fingers with a hint of vanilla catching in my nose. Pulling the sleeve of my hoodie over my hand, I polish her shoes, wiping away the splatters.

The sweetest sound I've ever heard floats through the air like a dandelion on a summer breeze. "There's no harm done, please." She crouches beside me. "It was only water, wasn't it? It's not like you've made me all sticky." She sucks in a sharp breath. "With pop I mean. Like sticky with a sugary drink. You know?"

"Yes ma'am. Er, no ma'am." I block out the visions of making her sticky, and after staring for a moment, we both stand.

Her smile reaches her eyes, making them twinkle like the sun's rays bouncing off the waves.

"Can you help me? I'm looking for my cabin on deck six. Is that where you're headed?" She hands me a boarding ticket with her room number printed in bold lettering.

Nice, she's in one of the few Penthouse Veranda Staterooms they have on board. They're not cheap.

"This way." I point to the left, which takes us to the grand staircase. After working several ships over the last few years, I know my way around. "Let me help you with that." I take the Louis Vuitton carry-on case from her hand and walk beside her up the steps with my suitcase in the other.

"Thank you." Her smile pushes her rosy cheeks up, and she flutters her lashes at me.

An electric current charges through my body, forcing every cell to come alive. "Are you travelling alone?"

4

"Yes, it's just me, all on my billy."

My eyebrows pull together. "Who's Billy?"

"Billy-no-mates. Silly." She giggles, sending a vibration straight to my dick.

"I've never heard of him?" I haven't a clue what she's talking about, but I can't stop smiling.

Her hand knocks my arm. "It means I'm all alone, yes."

I chuckle. "Why not just say that, instead of bringing Billy into it?"

She's clearly British, with an accent like my ma's. Only, I don't have any motherly feelings for her. Quite the opposite.

A warmth spreads through my limbs as if electrons are travelling around a circuit board, lighting everything up in their wake. "Have you travelled far?"

"England."

I knew it. I search her hand for a ring but can't see even a ghost of one on her left hand.

I clear my throat as we approach the room. "Here we are. Room 6015." An expensive cabin to go with her expensive carry-on.

She swipes the lock with her card and opens the door to her luxurious accommodation. En suite, seating area, large bed and a balcony. A far cry from my room with no natural light source, shared with another crew member.

After placing her bag on top of the other two Louis Vuitton suitcases in the middle of the room, I watch her take in her new surroundings. She's wide-eyed like she's never seen the inside of a luxurious cabin before, which strikes me as odd that someone like her has never cruised.

She rushes to the balcony, her dress outlining her full

figure as she moves. A breath bottles up in my chest as I take in her excitement. She turns back to me, fluttering her lashes. "How do you open this balcony door?"

I walk over and pull the latch up. My fingers graze hers, and she sucks in a quick breath, then smiles. After I slide open the large patio glass doors, she steps out onto the balcony. The wind blows her curls, and she holds on to her hat. Her perfume floats through the air on the February breeze, and I inhale the vanilla scent in favour of the Los Angeles fish dock.

The view of the grimy port is before us, but her eyes sparkle, taking in the scene like a child seeing something for the first time. I lean against the railing with my hands in my pockets, in awe of her.

She turns back to me. "Where is your room? Are you here with your family? Or are you a solo traveller too?"

I huff out a laugh. "I like to travel alone."

She'll find out I work here soon enough. I guess I do look like any other tourist in my white tee, hoody, blue jeans, and Converse. I do have to get to work soon though and set up for the evening dining, but my feet won't move off this balcony.

"Would you like me to show you where anything else is, or should I leave you to unpack?"

"Oh no, I'm fine now, thank you. I'm just going to unpack my things and then get ready for orientation."

I nod and force my feet one in front of the other, not wanting to leave, but I shouldn't be here. The last thing I need is to get fired before my first shift. "I'll see you around." You can count on it.

"Bye and thank you again."

LIZZIE

A FLUTTER in my heart confuses me as he strolls out the door, turns back and flashes a grin, making the scar above his lip more prominent.

I wanted to ask him what happened. My brother has a similar scar on his nose from a dog bite when he was young. Maybe I'll get to ask him the next time I see him. I'm bound to bump into him again on the ship in such close proximity. The thought of seeing him again fills me with a warm fuzziness, making me think of bumping uglies. Is that the phrase these days?

I take my overly large sun hat from my head and place it on the dressing table. Flopping back on the huge bed, I starfish. Doing a double roll to the side, I pull my phone from my bag and call my brother and his wife while I still have a phone signal.

My sister-in-law, Susie, answers. "Lizzie. How is it?"

"It's wonderful. Everything is so luxurious, no expense spared." I glance around my room with a smile on my face.

"I'm so happy for you." Susie squeals down the phone. "You deserve this after everything you've been through lately. I want you to forget about everything and enjoy yourself. Maybe have a little fun too, hmm?"

"No. No men. I've sworn off men… well, I had until about fifteen minutes ago when a cute guy helped me find my cabin."

7

"What's his name? Tell me everything."

I chew on the inside of my mouth, realising I didn't get his name. "Er, I don't know. I didn't actually find anything out about him, other than he's travelling alone too."

"A man of mystery. I like the sound of that."

I twirl a lock of hair around my finger while gazing at the white cabin ceiling. "He was sort of mysterious and ruggedly handsome, with a scar above his lip."

"Swoon, I'm getting James Bond, Daniel Craig vibes. You should definitely get to know him."

"No. I've come on this holiday to get away from all that loved-up nonsense."

"You're on a Valentine's cruise." She giggles.

"I know, I know, this is a Valentine's cruise, but beggars can't be choosers." It seems wherever I go, there's no escaping it, but anything is better than watching my brother and Susie—along with my friends—get spoilt by their partners on Valentine's. Not that Dwayne ever spoilt me. He was always a selfish prick.

"It's the first Valentine's you've been single in years. Have some fun."

"I'll do my best. Why I ever stayed with him for so long, I'll never know."

"Good riddance, that's what I say. He can keep his little floozy behind the bar. The best thing you ever did was leave him and that small town country pub."

"Thanks, Susie. How is Eddie?"

"We're all good here. Enjoy yourself, and we'll see you in two weeks. Send me pictures of any hot billionaires you meet. I can live vicariously through you."

I giggle. "Okay. See you soon. Love you."

"Love you, too. Bye."

I look out at the LA harbour and tall buildings in the distance, inhaling the fresh sea breeze mixed with that city life scent.

There's a rumbling from the depths of the boat and faint music from a brass band drifting up from the docks. My tummy flutters again as the boat comes to life, and I'm about to embark on my first adventure.

After unpacking, I step into the corridor, closing the door behind me. A girl steps out of the next room.

"Hey, neighbour," she says in a strong American accent.

"Hello, I'm Elizabeth. Nice to meet you."

She gives me a friendly smile. "Kenna, you too."

I pull a map of the ship from my bag. "I'm on my way to this orientation thing, but I'm not entirely sure where to go."

"Me too. Follow me, I know the way." Kenna and I walk side by side down the small corridor. With my heels on, I tower over her small curvy frame.

Her tight black curls spiral around her face, bouncing as we walk. "Are you here alone?"

Why does everyone keep asking me that? Is it so unusual for a woman to travel alone? "Yes, what about you?"

"Yep, I'm actually here for work. I'm writing an article about the maiden voyage to Hawaii. This cruise line has been in hot water with the press lately, and the media company I work for wanted someone on board who could accurately report on any mishaps."

"Oh, I do hope there are no mishaps. This is my first

holiday in years."

We step into the elevator as Kenna explains, "Deck six and seven orientations are in the Navigator's Lounge. I did a lot of research before getting here, so I know where everything is. Stick with me, babe, and you'll never be lost."

I laugh as the elevator door dings. "Prepare to become my best friend then, because I'd get lost in my own apartment."

Once in the lounge, I look around, searching for my mystery man. Darn, why didn't I get his name? He's not here, just a room full of loved up couples, holding hands and cuddling. Ugh, makes me sick. I know I'm on a Valentine's cruise, but still. Kenna nudges me and points to a big muscly guy.

I shrug. "He's hot, but not really my type. I like more slender men."

Kenna waggles her eyebrows and scans the room while my mind drifts. Although Dwayne was skinny, he thought he was God's gift—the arrogant twat. I huff through my nostrils, thinking of him. It's been a few months, but he still gets my back up. I'm not sure what hurt more, losing him or being rejected.

The feeling of worthlessness when I caught him with her refuses to leave, but underneath is anger burning into bitterness. I screw my face up like I can taste the infidelity on my tongue.

I know I deserve so much more. I'll never let another man treat me that way again. From now on, I call the shots. I did everything for him, too—ungrateful shit.

I'm snapped from my thoughts when a red-headed

woman speaks to the group, introducing herself as Roxanne. I try not to yawn, listening to the safety briefing. It's been a long day. The flight from England to LA last night wasn't very comfortable with little sleep. A couple to my right bicker, bringing my attention back to the briefing. I smile at the drama, happy to see not everyone is as lovey-dovey as I thought.

CHAPTER Two

ZAC

ONCE CHANGED into my shirt and slacks, I straighten my bowtie and attach my name badge. I run a blob of gel through my brown hair, wrinkling my brow as I style it in the mirror, trying to get this curl to go in the right direction. Though the ladies go nuts for this bit of hair that falls over onto my forehead, it annoys the hell out of me.

I could do with a shave, but the five o'clock shadow seems to be a hit with the girls too, so I leave it. A splash of cologne, and I'm ready for work. I place the Versace bottle back on the bathroom shelf in my small crew cabin. It was a gift from a passenger on the Christmas cruise. One of many gifts I received. Most people think I have it cushy doing this job, but keeping a smile on my face and flirting back to be polite can be a real headache, especially when you find out later that they're married.

Arriving at the Italian restaurant for my shift, I check the bookings and see Cabin 6015. Her name sits next to the number. Elizabeth Rose Jones. Even her name oozes sophistication. I'll earn a shitload of tips from her if I play my cards right. Fuck, I sound like my pa. That's not me, but being treated like dirt repeatedly by rich folk, it's hard to see past a bank account sometimes.

She didn't seem like all the others, though. Sure, her cabin, clothes, and luggage all cried out wealth, but something gleamed in her eyes that wasn't like them. Maybe she's won the lottery. Who cares? I won't be seeing her after this cruise, and there'll be another set of rich desperados to entertain. The sooner I've saved up enough money to set up on my own, the better.

The restaurant fills, and the once quiet room becomes a den of chatter, clinking glasses, and cutlery. As I serve the guests, her table is still empty. I wonder what's keeping her. The aroma of Italian cuisine wafts through from the galley, taking me back to my childhood and my grandparents' Italian restaurant.

I'm brought back to the present with a sharp jolt to my chest when I turn to see a woman in blue walk to her seat. The seat I've had my eye on all evening. Her dress comes above the knee, showing a hint of those meaty thighs. The fabric curves around her bust, giving me a glimpse of cleavage I could lose myself in.

I close my mouth, grab a menu, and walk over to alleviate Josh from his duty. "I'll take care of this table."

Josh rolls his eyes and walks away. I hand Elizabeth a menu, and she widens her smile, sitting down before me.

"You work here?" She squints her eyes as she studies my name badge. "Zachary Walters?"

Hearing my name roll off her tongue soothes my soul, like listening to the gentle waves of the ocean. "Call me Zac. Nice to meet you again."

"I'm sorry. I thought you were a guest. Should I have tipped you earlier? I'm still not sure how tipping works in the States, or on this ship."

My head tilts to side, taking in her confession. "No, ma'am, I was off duty earlier. No need for a tip." Where has she lived, Mars? No, England. "I'll come back in a few minutes to take your order. What can I get you to drink?"

"I'll just have a rosé wine, please."

"Will that be the Laurent Perrier Cuvee Rosé or a Chateau d'Esclans Cotes de Provence?" I grab the pen and notepad from my pocket, ready to jot down her favourite drink.

She peruses the drinks menu, wrinkling her forehead as her eyes dilate. "I'll have the rosé house wine, please."

My head jerks back. I was about to say my usual spiel about what an excellent choice she's made, but I'd hardly call the house wine a good choice. "Shall I bring the bottle?"

She glances at the menu one more time and smiles. "Yes, why not?"

I wink as I leave the table to get her drink and she sucks in a breath.

Josh is behind the bar pouring drinks. "I thought you'd like her, although she's not as old as the ones you usually go for."

"All right, dickhead. At least all the women I flirt with are of legal age."

He narrows his eyes at me, able to dish it out but not take it. The guys on my last ship were jealous because I got the most tips, but that's because I served the right clients.

I take her drink to the table and, standing over her, I pour a little into her glass. "Madam."

She shakes her head, causing her golden curled hair to fall in front of her left shoulder and a loose strand follows the curve down to her cleavage. "I don't need to try it. Just top it up; it's fine."

A smile plays on my lips. She's my kinda woman. A small heart and a delicate swallow tattoo catch my eye, peeking out from under the strap of her dress. My fingers itch to reveal more and see what else she has written on her sinful body. After staring for a beat too long, I pour the wine into her glass, filling it up as she asked.

Her eyes are on my tattooed wrist where the cuff of my shirt has ridden up.

"Nice tat."

My lips curve into a grin. "Thanks. You have nice tits as well."

I freeze. My throat grows thick and sweat breaks out on my forehead. "I mean tats. Fuck. Tats. I'm sorry, ma'am."

I knock the wine glass. It falls in slow motion and clatters against the silverware, spilling the rosé on the crisp white tablecloth. My hand fumbles with a napkin, mopping up the spill. Just keep calm. Damn it, I was trying to flirt with her, not insult her. At least it didn't spill on her dress, or I would be in trouble.

She giggles and picks up the empty glass. Our fingers touch, and I suck in a quick gulp of air as an electrical charge surges through my bloodstream.

"Please, forgive me, ma'am. I didn't mean to say that they were nice." Just stop fucking talking. What's wrong with you? Fucking idiot.

Her hand covers mine, steadying my fumbling hand. "Are you saying I *don't* have nice breasts?" Her eyes twinkle, mesmerising me like the ocean. Waiting for my response, she cocks an eyebrow and bites her lip.

I relax a little and brush the shell of her ear with my lips. "Your tits are fucking perfect."

She giggles, and it's the sweetest sound. What's wrong with me? I straighten and wink. "I'll get you another bottle, ma'am."

Her hand grips my wrist before I walk away. "Call me Lizzie."

I nod and rush towards the bar, shaking my head. What an idiot. Although she didn't seem to mind.

"Josh, I'm gonna need another bottle of rosé."

Josh grabs a bottle from the cooler. "What table?" He's about to charge for it.

"On the house. I spilled a drink."

He nods. "You're not just trying to impress the ladies again, are you?"

"You know me, but I did genuinely knock over a drink. I was distracted."

Jiggling two wine bottles in front of his chest, he says, "I think I can guess what distracted you."

I snatch the bottle and make my way back to the table. Keep your cool. Just stay cool. As I approach, I catch her laughing with another guest who's joined her. Pouring the fresh drink, I concentrate on the glass in my hand instead of her cleavage. "There you go ma'am. I mean, Lizzie."

Her hand grazes mine as she takes the glass from me, sending an army of goosebumps marching up my arm. The hairs on the back of my neck stand to attention when she speaks.

"Thank you, Zac." The smile pushing her blush cheeks up causes a stutter in my chest. This woman is gonna ruin me.

LIZZIE

AFTER BREAKFAST, I change into my red swimsuit with a frilled skirt attached, covering my large bottom and the top of my dimply thighs. As confident as I am with my body, I thought this swimsuit was cute, accentuating my assets with a low-cut neck that dips open at the cleavage.

I place my sunglasses on my head, cover myself with a kimono, and grab my hat and bag before heading to the poolside.

The infinity pool is small, but less busy than the main pool. A clear shield surrounds the area, protecting me from the sea wind, but still allows me to see the gentle lapping of the ocean. I pull out my towel and cover the lounger before relaxing on my back and opening my magazine from the airport.

Flicking through all the usual makeup tips, I come across an article, 'Golden Penis Syndrome.' Of course I'm curious. Apparently it's where the guy ratio to girls is in their favour, and they basically get more attention than they should, giving them an over inflated ego.

I snort. Dwayne definitely had this. I flick the page, not being arsed to read anything that would remind me of that pathetic loser, and spy an article titled, 'I went on a cruise to f*ck strangers in front of my husband.'

Oh my, does this sort of thing go on? My back sweats, so I straighten, pick my sun hat from the bag, and tuck my hair inside. Crossing my legs, I continue to read the article with wide eyes, lost in this scandalous world.

"Hello, Lizzie."

A warm breath lands on my neck, sending a cascade of tingles down my spine. When I turn, I see a grin as wide as the ship's hull.

"Interesting article." Zac quirks an eyebrow, chuckling as he takes the sun lounger next to mine and pulls off his white t-shirt, leaving him in nothing but his Hawaiian swim shorts.

I glance around to see who he's with, but he's alone. My eyes scan his tattooed sleeve. Black ink details the inside of a robot, like something from the 'Terminator' covering his forearm.

He unfurls the towel he was carrying, letting a bottle of sun cream fall out. The smell of coconut floats through the air as he lathers it over his sun-kissed skin. A swallow tattoo decorating the left of his chest catches my eye, and I gasp, because the ink resembles mine.

After gazing at his delectable body for several minutes, he waves a hand towards my magazine. "Don't mind me, carry on reading your porn mag."

His grin is infectious, but I bite the inside of my mouth to stop from breaking into a smile.

"It isn't porn."

"What is it then?"

"Cosmo." I unfold the magazine and show him the cover.

He laughs.

I frown. "What's so funny?"

"Nothing." He's still chuckling.

I roll the magazine up and reach over to swat his chest with it, but before I can hit him, his hand grips the paper. He takes it from me and flicks through, stopping to read. "How to get the best orgasm with Bob." He looks up at me. "Who's Bob? Is he a friend of Billy's?"

I roll my eyes. "Battery operated boyfriend. The only boyfriend worth having, if you ask me."

"Maybe I should start reading Cosmo."

I snatch it back. "Get your own magazine."

He chuckles again. "You clearly haven't been with a real man if you prefer Bob."

"When you spot one, be sure to point him out." I curl the corner of my mouth into a smile and bite my lip.

He lowers himself onto his chest, lying down on the sun lounger with a cocky grin as he twists his neck to face me. "Take off those sunglasses, and you'll see a real man."

My head snaps to the side. Not another arrogant arse. "Are you even allowed up here? Shouldn't you be at work?"

"I start at one today. And no, not allowed, but seeing you is worth the risk."

"How did you know I was here?" My head tilts, wondering if this is a coincidence or if he planned to meet me here.

"I heard you tell your friend you were going to relax by the pool today, so I thought I'd join you. Do you mind?"

I blink rapidly. So he did plan it. "No, no, not at all. It's nice to have some company." Heat prickles my skin and claws its way up my neck. He's very attractive, and I do fancy him, which is the problem. I'm not ready to get my heart broken again and with a two-week holiday fling, that's exactly what will happen. Inhaling a deep breath, I give my head a shake, telling myself I must resist him. Besides, looks aren't what I go for—I like a man that can make me laugh—anyone who saw my ex would vouch for that. Only by the end of our relationship I wasn't laughing.

Zac holds the sun cream out to me. "Would you do my back?"

I draw in a breath, and glance around, checking he was talking to me.

"I don't bite," he says with a grin. "I lick."

"Ugh, please. You suck, you mean."

"That too."

I giggle. He got me there. "Fine."

With a knotted stomach, I take the bottle from him and squeeze the cream into my hand, inhaling the luscious smell that encompasses holiday. He scoots his body over a little and pats the sun lounger for me to sit next to him.

The small space is only big enough for one arse cheek, so I squat, resting half my bottom there as I rub the cream over the ink on his shoulder.

A few cogs spill over from his bicep, leaving the rest of his back clear. He flexes his shoulders, making the muscles move against my palms and a flicker warms the pit of my stomach, like he's turned on a switch that buzzes in my core.

He exhales a long breath as he relaxes under my massaging hands. "I could get used to this."

"I'm sure you're already used to this. Is this how you flirt with all the girls?"

He turns his head to me and winks. "Only the pretty ones."

The buzz low in my belly intensifies, and I clench my thighs together to stop the dampness pooling there. Beads of moisture coat my skin and the water has never looked so inviting.

After working the lotion into his lower back, I slide my hand along the elastic waistband of his shorts, wishing I could go lower and squeeze his toned arse. Before I have any more ideas, I force my hands from his skin. "All done."

"Thanks."

My legs won't move and after sitting awkwardly on his sun lounger, I have a serious case of pins and needles. I can't seem to get myself off the bed with one numb leg. I wobble like a Weeble, trying to propel myself up.

His head tilts with pinched eyebrows. "What are you doing?"

I wince as the tingles in my leg multiply, and life comes back into my foot.

"Pins and needles." I say, holding my leg out.

He sits up, takes my calf between his warm hands and massages from my knee down to my foot. His vibrant green eyes appear brighter with the sun's rays shining on them, highlighting another scar on his temple that wrinkles when he smiles.

I lean back on his sun lounger as he works my numb muscles, bringing new life back into them with each stroke of his fingers. The tingles shoot from my leg straight to where all my nerves meet at that little spot between my thighs.

His skin still glistens from the lathering of sun cream, and I want to rub it in his chest some more. I shake the thought, chanting in my head, I don't want a man, I don't want a man, but my heart thrums a different beat, causing my breath to quicken.

His eyes lower onto my mouth, then to my chest. He licks his lips, staring at my cleavage, while digging his fingers into my fleshy calf. He said my breasts were perfect last night, but he's perfect. Everything about him is perfect, and I feel my walls crumbling with each look, touch, and word from him.

I snap my head away, then my leg. "I'm okay now. Thank you." I can't allow myself to get involved.

With the desperate need to cool off, I drop my hat on my sun bed and walk to the edge of the pool, welcoming the chilled temperature as I climb down the steps. The water creeps up my thighs and eventually hits the spot between my legs, taking the heat there down a few notches. Bending my knees, I push off the side into the breast stroke and glance over at Zac, watching me with a grin still on his face.

His hair flops over his forehead but isn't long enough to reach his eyes. I wonder what the time is and how much longer I have with him before he has to go to work. I'll cool off, then return to chat with him some more.

# CHAPTER
Three

ZAC

WATCHING her in the pool has my cock growing another inch. He was already awake when she started rubbing lotion on my back, but seeing her dripping wet hair slicked back off her face, and her tits in that red swimsuit, bouncing in the water like two buoys keeping her afloat, has me salivating.

Down boy, I say to myself, but he doesn't listen. I want to join her in the pool, but if I stand now, everyone will see my throbbing dick.

Makani comes over. "I see you haven't changed. Up to your usual tricks again, Zac?"

"I don't know what you're talking about." We worked together on another cruise over a year ago and he thinks he knows me.

He shakes his head and snickers, collecting empty glasses by the pool. Lizzie swims to the side and places her arms on the tiled edge. "Excuse me, could I have a drink, please?"

"Certainly ma'am. What can I get you?"

"A mocktail, please, something refreshing. I'll let you choose."

"And what room number and name?"

"6015, Miss Jones."

"She'll have a Virgin Mai Tai and I'll have a Maui Mocktail, please." I wink at Makani. He glares back at me before marching back to the bar. He's probably jealous I'm hanging out with this stunning, affluent woman. I know he didn't just walk over here to collect two empty glasses.

Lizzie pinches her eyebrows and tuts at me from the pool. "I might not have wanted that?"

"You were gonna let Makani choose. I thought I'd at least get you something you'll like."

"How do you know I'll like it?"

"Trust me."

"I don't trust any man." She pushes on the side and swims in the opposite direction.

Sounds like she's been hurt in the past. I wonder what happened to her. There's a tug on my heartstrings as if someone is playing a harp, only it's a sad tune, making me want to protect her and make her feel loved again. I know how rejection feels; there's nothing worse than your pa walking out on you.

After Makani's presence, it didn't take long for my dick to retreat, and I take a few steps towards the edge of the water and jump in, splashing her in the process. She blinks the water from her eyes as I swim close to her.

She treads water, still blinking. Her chin bobs up and down with the small rippling waves. "Are you always this annoying?"

I chuckle. "Are you always this snarky?"

She juts her chin out. "Only with annoying waiters."

There's a sparkle in her eyes, matching the blue topaz

jewel around her neck, and a smile playing on her lips that tells me she means only with waiters she wants to fuck. She likes the attention, and I think she likes me. I know she likes me.

Treading water in the middle of the pool, I move closer. "Tell me, what's a woman like you doing travelling alone?"

She shrugs. "I'm a big girl. I can do whatever I want."

I quirk a grin. She knows that's not what I meant.

Makani comes back with our drinks, and my eyes flick to the sunlit sky. Fucking perfect timing as always. I climb out of the pool in one swift jump, my shorts dripping along the dry deck as I take both drinks and make my way over to the hot tub.

Her eyebrows pinch together. She doesn't appreciate being bossed around, but most women love a man that takes care of their every need—don't they?

"I'll leave the receipt here for you, ma'am," Makani says, placing the drinks receipt on her sun lounger, tucked under her hat before walking back to the bar.

"Are you coming in, Lizzie?"

She gives me an eye roll, but swims to the steps. The water runs off her body and the sun shines on her, making her skin sparkle like she's something from a vampire movie. Only I'm the predator.

I place the drinks on the tiled floor next to the hot tub, lean back, and take in every curve as she flexes out of the pool. Rivulets descend her silky smooth skin, dripping from her hair, making my mouth water as if sucking on candy.

My eyes move to her meaty hips when they come out

of the pool and I lick my lips, thinking how I'd love to dig my fingers into that flesh while pounding into her. The red swimsuit rides up between her ass, giving me the perfect view of her plump, supple cheeks, like a large juicy peach I could sink my teeth into.

She stands and pulls at the lycra skirt attached to her swimsuit, letting it fall around the tops of her thick thighs, but not before I notice the dainty garter tattoo at the top of her leg. It's cute with black lace detail and a pink bow in the centre.

I smile and so does my dick, nodding in agreement. She's sexy as fuck. My mouth is still open as she steps into the sunken tub. The water bubbles all around me, popping and gurgling along with the hum of the pump.

She misses the step and stumbles down. I hurry to catch her, but she forces me back against the seat, almost straddling me. My chest tightens and my breath quickens as my gaze drops to her plush chest in my face. A lump lodges in my throat when I see my hand is on her tit. Fuck. My hand is on her *tit*.

With a slack jaw she widens her eyes at me and I swiftly move my hand down to her hip while she gets her balance, making sure I don't grab her ass this time, even though I'd love to squeeze those succulent cheeks under her lycra swimsuit.

The jets pumping air underneath us prevent her from gaining her balance and her hands grip my shoulders. I contemplate pulling her closer to steal a kiss, but I fear she would slap me. Plus, I can't get involved with a guest. There are too many people here. 'Flirt and show the single ladies a good time, but no hanky-panky' are the boss's words.

She stares at me with eyes like a frozen lake. Each time she takes a deep panting breath, her lip quivers, matching my trembling hand as I hold her.

"Are you falling for me already?"

She pushes herself from me. The heat from the tub rises, painting her cheeks a beautiful shade of rose. Once settled in the seat next to me, she says. "You didn't just say that? It's so corny."

"There's plenty more where that came from, sweetheart."

She huffs. "Please, spare me."

With a chuckle, I reach for her drink. "Here, get your drink and shut up."

"Ugh, you're so charming." She takes the orange and yellow mocktail garnished with a pineapple wedge and two cherries.

I raise an eyebrow. "I can show you charming, princess."

Taking my yellow Maui Mocktail, I suck up the cool fruity liquid, take out the pink flower that dangles from the side of the glass next to a wedge of pineapple, and tuck it behind her ear. She doesn't need it, though. She's beautiful all on her own, but she compliments the flower.

"Try your drink. Do you like it?"

She sips through the straw. "It's nice."

"You can thank me later."

She rolls her eyes again. "Ugh, you're relentless. Don't you have to be at work yet?" A smile tugs at the corner of her mouth, making me want to smother it with my lips.

"Don't worry, you have me for another hour." I give her a wink and love how she acts like she hates it.

"Thrilling," she says in a sarcastic tone with a sassy eyeball.

"I love how confident you are."

A long sigh leaves her lips with a low rumbling groan as she slumps and inches away.

"What's wrong? Don't you like a compliment?" I suck the fruity mocktail that's giving me a sugar high. Or is it her?

"Not a back-handed one like that."

"How was that backhanded? What's wrong with being confident?"

"I know what you meant." She mocks in my voice. "I love how confident you are for a big girl."

Whoa, that came out of nowhere. Sitting up straight, I slide towards her, closing the gap between us. "I meant no such thing. I love how confident you are. Period."

She pulls her head back, blinking. "Oh. Thanks." She sips her drink and relaxes next to me again, brushing her arm with mine.

"And for the record, I love a girl with big—"

Her head tilts towards me, and I smirk, nodding at her ripe melons. She lowers herself further into the water so the bubbles cover the crevice where my eyes rest.

"Yes, you made it clear last night what you thought about...those." Her tongue circles the straw in her drink while she inspects my swallow tattoo.

I rub my hand over the ink. "You like it?"

She nods. "I have the same one." She turns her shoulder and moves her hair to show me the design.

"I know. I saw it last night." My fingers are itching to trace the outline, or better still, trace it with my tongue. I wonder what other little surprises she has under that swimsuit.

She points to my chest. "What does yours represent?"

"Freedom."

She giggles. "Why? Have you been in prison?"

"No. Have you?" I tease.

The ice at the bottom of her glass rattles as she fiddles with the straw. "I got my swallow recently. It represents loyalty."

"So, who are you loyal to?"

"Myself. It's a reminder I will never let another man walk all over me like my ex did, hence only one bird. When I meet 'the one', I'll add another to join it, but until I find someone worthy, this bird's flying solo."

I rub my inked chest. Maybe this could be 'the one' to match it. They're not identical in design, but close enough. Mine is swooping down, and hers is looking up as if waiting for me to meet her, just like her lips now. A loose strand of wet hair sticks to her cheek, and my fingers graze her skin, gently tucking it behind her ear with the flower I placed there a moment ago.

My stomach flips like a pod of dolphins at play. I've never let a guest get to me like this before. My head jolts back before I do something I'll regret, and I take another drink to quench my dry throat. The steam from the hot tub billows around us, but I'm hotter than a boiled lobster, and probably just as red.

I need to keep my cool. She's here for a good time, and I'm here to earn money for my restaurant. Sleeping with a guest would jeopardise my dream. Logically I know that, but something about her makes me feel better than I have in a long time and it's hard to turn that down. I can tell by the way she looks at me, she feels the same, but she's fighting this connection, too.

CHAPTER Four

LIZZIE

I UNPACK my bag from yesterday, looking for my necklace. Did I even take it off? I was so caught up with Zac I don't remember if I took it off before getting into the pool. My chest tightens, and my skin breaks out in a sweat. There's no necklace in my bag, but I find several drinks receipts for the mocktails I had.

Wanting to know the name of the ones Zac ordered for me, I study each one. Not only are my drinks listed, but his as well. His drinks have been charged to my room, the cheeky twat. Why am I smiling? Hmm, and why would Makani assume it was okay to put his drinks on my tab? Maybe it was a mistake. I screw the receipts up and toss them in the bin. Oh well, not to worry. I have plenty of spending money, but he can get the drinks next time. The thought of spending another day with him gives me a delightful shiver. I hope I see him again today. Maybe he can tell me if he remembers seeing a necklace.

Arriving at the Italian restaurant for the workshop, a small group of us are taken into the kitchen and shown to a workstation. I stand in front of the bench, picking up a white apron in my hands like I'm about to take part in the TV show, 'The Great British Bake Off'.

Zac walks towards me in his waistcoat with his name badge on. He smiles when our eyes meet, and I think my heart just stopped for a second.

He stands next to me. "Hi, I was hoping I'd see you here." Taking the apron from my hands, he pops it on over my head and ties the strings at the back of my waist. I let him, not able to speak or think in his presence.

An Italian guy stands at the front of the room. "Afternoon, ladies and gentlemen. My name is Giovanni, and I'm the pastry chef here aboard the Serenade. Welcome to the workshop. Today we will make Cannoli. Our crew members are on hand to assist you."

Zac winks, making my stomach muscles pull inwards. Is he going to be my partner? Another flip in my stomach as he checks we have all the correct pots, utensils, and ingredients.

Giovanni continues to instruct us from the front of the galley.

I bring the bowl in front of my belly while Zac weighs the flour. "So, what do you do, Lizzie, when you're back home in England?"

"Er." I pause for a moment, thinking of what to say. "I run a bar."

"Nice."

I smile, pouring the flour into the bowl. "It was okay. I mean, it is okay."

"So, what would you rather be doing? When you're not hanging out on cruise ships?"

I shrug a shoulder and pick up the sugar. "I've always wanted to own a coffee shop."

His eyes grow wide. "My dream is to open an Italian restaurant."

"Are you Italian?"

He pours the bicarbonate of soda into the mix. "My grandfather was Italian. He emigrated to the States in his twenties, met my grandmama, and they owned an Italian restaurant." His eyes twinkle like the emerald city when he talks about his grandparents. I add the cinnamon and cocoa while he sprinkles a bit of salt into the mixture.

After scraping the butter into the bowl, I search for a utensil.

"Use your hands," Zac says. "Like this." He takes my hands and places them in the bowl, massaging my fingers as he squeezes the mixture together. He's so close. The fresh pine tree scent he wears catches in my nose, reminding me of home. With each stroke of his thumb against my palm, a tingle surges through to my core.

His large hands engulf mine as he interlaces our fingers. Turning his head slightly, he peers into my eyes. Time slows down, the kitchen blurs, and all I see are his eyes, dark and dense like a forest of unruly foliage.

My head snaps away from his gaze when Giovanni speaks again. "Once your mixture is combined, add the egg yolk and Marsala to the bowl."

Still rubbing his hands over mine in the mixture, Zac says, "Are you ready?"

I gulp, gazing back into his eyes. "Ready for what?"

"To add the eggs?"

"Oh. Yes. Of course." Each time I gaze into his eyes, I'm pulled deeper into the forest, making it harder to find my way back.

He releases my hands, and I pick up the egg and crack it into a separate container. "How do I separate these?"

Zac delves into the jug and pulls out the yolk, letting the egg white run between his fingers. He tips it into the jar that holds the Marsala wine, and I mix it with a small whisk and pour it into the bowl. Zac takes my hands again, and we knead the mixture together. "So how long have you been single?"

I glance at him with my eyebrows squished. "Not long enough."

"That bad, huh?"

"Yes. I don't want another man."

"Maybe I can change your mind." He holds my hand in his and stops kneading for a moment, sending another surge of heat down to my core. Stop it, I tell myself, not wanting to get attached. After all, I won't see him again after this holiday. *Isn't that a good thing?* Maybe.

"So, why are you single?"

"I hate all men."

He smirks. "Really?"

"Well, I make exceptions for waiters." I flash him a smile and glance up at him through my lashes. His grin matches mine, and I'm lost once more in those evergreens.

"Is that all waiters, or just one in particular?" His fingers interlace with mine again under the mixture.

I pause for a moment, chewing on the inside of my mouth. "Hmm, one waiter in particular that works in an Italian restaurant on a cruise ship."

His grin spreads as he massages my hands.

What am I doing? I have sworn off men. Nope, I'm not

getting into this. *You're flirting, not marrying the guy. Have a bit of fun.* Is that my vagina talking? I squeeze my thighs together, hoping to shut her up, and smile at Zac. "It's that blonde guy you were working with last night. What's his name again?"

He chuckles. Pulling his hands away, playfully knocking my shoulder, then his hand knocks over a bag of icing sugar.

ZAC

Fuuuck. I look down at my dick covered in a fine white powder, highlighting the fact that I'm hard as a rock. Lizzie sucks in a breath. Her eyes dart to my dick and practically pop their sockets. She stares at my bulging crotch with her mouth open.

Removing her hands from the bowl, she grabs a cloth and dusts down my slacks, unintentionally rubbing me, but with each swipe of her hand, my cock twitches. Another minute of this, and she'll be cleaning up more than icing sugar.

"Lizzie, I got this," I growl, taking the cloth from her to dust myself off. A cloud of sugar whirls around my feet, and I can taste the sweetness in the air. Luckily, it wasn't the full bag, but a bit of that stuff goes a long way, coating the bench in a fine white dusting.

Why does she make me so clumsy? I don't normally

get this way around women, even beautiful women like her. I see them every day on the ship, but she makes me go weak. One look is all it takes and my cock comes alive.

She glances at me with a giggle and knocks my arm.

I want to kiss that mouth of hers and swallow those cute giggles up. What's wrong with me? *Keep your head in the game, Zac. Don't fuck with the guests.* I never get attached to guests like this, and fuck, it's only been three days.

Giovanni walks around the workstations. "Everything okay, sì?" he asks in his thick Italian accent. I nod, still dusting my black pants down that are now grey. He walks away laughing under his breath—the jerk—then continues with his instructions.

I try to tune in to Giovanni, but Lizzie is too damn distracting. It's a good thing I've made these a million times with my grandparents. "How's it feeling now?"

She squishes the dough with her fingers. "I don't know. What do you think?"

I take over, dropping the dough onto the bench, then knead and roll under my palms.

Her wide eyes gaze into mine. "Has it gone soft?"

I clear my throat. Is she talking about this dough or my dick? "Do you want to take over?"

"Only if you will help me again." She flutters her eyelashes at me and smiles. She doesn't need to ask twice. I take her hands in mine, she palms the dough, while I palm the back of her soft hands, imagining them on my body.

I breathe in the honey fragrance of her shampoo, and a hint of coconut from her sunscreen. "Let's wrap this up now."

I don't want to stop touching her hands, but this dough will be overworked if I continue. We cover up the mixture, and I place it in the large fridge.

After washing, we walk through the galley and into the restaurant where a selection of miniature cakes, tea, and coffee is available.

"I'll help serve the other guests, then I'll come and sit with you."

She nods and fills a plate.

Once everyone's settled, I take a break, pour two coffees and sit at her table. She pushes the plate of cakes over to the middle, and I bite into a mini paradise bun, tasting the vanilla and peanut flavour on my tongue.

She sips her coffee. "Tell me more about this Italian restaurant you plan on owning one day."

"I'm saving up. By the end of this year, I'll have enough money to put a deposit on a place and go to night classes, finish culinary school and then apply for my licence."

She listens as I go on about cooking and my grandparents' restaurant. Like really listens. None of the other women I've talked to about my dreams have ever listened so intently. Usually they glaze over, wanting to talk about them. But she not only listens, she asks questions. I could talk to her for hours like this. She has one of those voices that's soft and caring and makes you feel valued.

"Anyway, tell me about you. Why do you hate all men...apart from sexy waiters?" I grin and take a drink of my coffee.

Her cheeks turn a beautiful shade of blush as she

giggles and looks down like she's embarrassed or something. Using my finger and thumb, I reach over and lift her chin to look at me and then tuck a loose blonde strand of hair back behind her ear.

"My ex cheated on me."

My brow wrinkles. Why would anyone cheat on her? "I'm sorry you went through that."

She shrugs. "It's okay. I'm over it. To think, I practically ran that bar and the whole time he was having it away with a server in the stockroom."

"What an idiot."

"The worst part was, she was my friend, but they deserve each other. Anyway, I don't want to talk about them. They make me nauseous."

"Noted. Let's talk about this hot waiter you're into."

She giggles again. "The blonde guy? You still haven't told me his name."

"The only name you need to know is mine, because it's what you'll be screaming by the end of the week."

She spits out her coffee, then coughs like she's choking, trying to clear her throat. Her face is as red as the raspberries on the cakes. Why did I say that? I can't control my mouth when I'm around her. That would end my contract with the ship, but it was totally worth it to see the look on her face.

"You're so cliché." Her eyes dramatically roll, but a smile plays on her lips and I can tell she's fighting it. "I'm not looking for another relationship, Zac."

"Good, because neither am I."

Her head tilts to the side. She stares at me, taking in what I just said.

"I only said you would be screaming my name, not saying *I do* in front of an altar."

"I'm not that sort of girl."

"What type of girl is that? One that doesn't scream or one that doesn't like a good screwing?"

"I'm not having this conversation with you. You're far too cocky for your own good."

I chuckle. Although I'm shocked at myself, I rarely take things this far. I shouldn't make promises I can't keep. I need this job. The last thing I want is to get canned for fooling around with the guests. Though, if she took me up on my offer, I don't think I could refuse.

"You like my cocky attitude, though." I lean across the table and whisper into her ear, "Or is it my cock? You couldn't take your eyes off it earlier."

She swats me away; her face the colour of beetroot now.

I back up, knocking my drink over as I retreat. Shit. She smirks as I grab the napkin and mop up the coffee.

"That's the third time you've had a spillage with me."

"Next time it will be more than a spill." I growl. "It'll be an eruption."

"Keep up your cocky attitude and next time, I'll tip it over your head." A giggle bursts from her mouth.

The sound travels straight to my dick and despite my clumsiness I'm hard again. "I'm sorry. I'm just messing with you. Staff aren't allowed to get involved with guests. HR rules."

"Oh." She slumps back in her seat, lowering her head while fiddling with the napkin. The brightness drains from her eyes as if a cloud has blocked out the sun.

Fuck. Way to go, dickhead. You certainly know how to kill the mood. "You're disappointed, aren't you?"

She straightens her back and shuffles in her seat, scrunching the napkin up on the table. "No. Why would I be? After all, I'm only here for a holiday."

I slide my hand over the table, almost touching hers. Electricity pulses between us, like magnets. Only she's repelling me, unsure and scared of getting hurt, perhaps. Who could blame her after what I just said? "Maybe I'll make an exception for a beautiful English rose."

The cloud in her eyes fades away, and her smile is back. "Rose is my middle name, after my mum."

"I saw it on the reservations. My middle name's Marco, after my nonno. When I get my restaurant, I'm calling it Marco's."

"That's a great name for an Italian. I'm sure your grandfather is proud of you." Her fingers move slightly, pulling towards mine, and the touch is barely visible, but I feel it with every cell in my body.

"Thanks."

"Oh, before I forget, did you see a necklace at the pool yesterday?"

"What necklace?" I search her neck for the jewel she was wearing yesterday.

"It's a blue teardrop topaz on a silver chain. It was my mother's."

"I haven't seen it, but you had it on when you were in the pool."

"I did?" Her face brightens, and her smile pushes her cheeks up.

"Yeah, I remember thinking it matched your eyes."

Two loud claps sound into the restaurant, and Giovanni ushers everyone back into the kitchen. "Now we deep fry the cannoli. Come."

CHAPTER *Five*

ZAC

I HAVEN'T SEEN Lizzie since the Italian Workshop yesterday. I had to cover a shift at the pyjama mixer party last night. Secretly, I hoped she would show up at the party in something sexy. Or even a onesie and bunny slippers like two girls there. That would have looked sexy on her too, like everything else I've seen her in.

When I arrive at work, the restaurant is full to the brim.

"Where have you been?" Josh asks, rushing to the bar with a notepad and pen in his hand.

"My shift doesn't start until 5pm."

He looks at his watch. "It's five minutes past."

"So, who are you, the time police?"

"Here. Get these for table twelve." He tears the drinks order from the pad, shoves it at me and rushes to serve another table.

I keep a lookout for Lizzie, knowing she usually comes for dinner around 7pm. We don't have any free tables, and I didn't see her name on the reservations for tonight. The restaurant is completely booked, and I'm busy the entire time, but I still can't help looking for her every five minutes like a love-struck schoolboy.

After my shift, I think about going to her room just to

check on her, but wonder if that's too stalkerish or desperate. Josh follows me out of the restaurant. "Hey, Zac. You coming for a beer?"

"Sure."

We walk below deck to the crew bar. Not as glamorous as upstairs, but it serves its purpose, and the music is much better than the stuff they play upstairs. Roland pours us both a cold one before we take a seat in a quiet corner with my roommate, Koa. "What's happenin'?"

"Hey, man. I'm just waiting for Roxy."

I sink into the couch next to Koa, taking a sip of the refreshing beer, and I rotate my shoulders and roll my neck, trying to relieve the tension from the day.

Josh pulls out a stool, sitting opposite. "Did you find that woman?"

"What woman?"

"The woman you've been pining for the last two days."

"Elizabeth? No, she didn't show up." I eye Koa, contemplating whether to ask for his help. "Can you slip a note into her room tomorrow? I want to spend the evening with her while I have some free time."

The big guy wipes his mouth. "You sure she's into you?"

"I think so." Taking in his reaction makes me question if she is into me or not, then I remember how she always lights up a room with her smile when she sees me. "No, I know so."

Josh chuckles. "She's done a good job of avoiding you. Perhaps you've lost your touch."

I roll my eyes and take a sip from the pint while

glancing around the dimly lit room. "If she isn't into me, she will be by the time I'm done."

"I feel a bet coming on." Josh rubs his hands together and nudges Koa with his elbow. "What you reckon, Koa?"

He shrugs. "I don't gamble, but I think you have your work cut out with that one."

"I can win her over, you'll see."

"What do you wanna bet?" Josh pulls out his wallet.

"I'm not betting fuck all. I'm not my pa. What happened to you telling me to lie low, anyway?"

"Bro, while you're pursuing the curvy blonde, you're not in any danger of getting into trouble. Can't get canned from someone who's not interested. Unless she files a restraining order." He puts his wallet away and they both laugh again.

I shake my head and snatch my drink from the table. Glancing over the pint as I guzzle it down, my eyes grow wide and I suck in a breath, causing the beer to go down the wrong hole. I cough, sputtering the liquid back out.

Koa pats my back, knocking the wind out of me. "You okay?"

My eyes water as I cough again, making my throat scratchy and I splutter out the words, "She's here."

Josh swings his head around, looking over his shoulder. "The curvy blonde? I don't see her."

"I wish. It's my ex, from the last ship I worked on." I turn away, sinking back into the couch. Maybe she won't notice me in this dark corner.

"Fuck, she's coming over," Josh says.

Jessica waltzes over to our table with a bottle in her hand. She flicks her blonde hair back over her shoulder and shoots me a deadly smile. I tuck my chin down. Talking to her is the last thing I want to do tonight, or ever for that matter. I hadn't even realised she was on this ship.

"Hello boys." She slithers her little bottom on the couch arm next to me. "Are you following me, Zac?" She tilts her head and sips her drink through a straw.

"Are *you* following *me*?" I give her a fake smile and squint my eyes slightly.

She lifts her bottom and slides closer to me, then glides her fingers up my forearm. "We can put all that behind us and start again."

I remove her hand that's making my skin crawl and place it on the table. "I'm good, thanks. It was fun while it lasted, but I'm not looking for a relationship." Not with you anyway, psycho.

"Let's have some fun, then." She reaches out and gently grazes her hand up my thigh, making my balls shrivel and my dick retreat the closer she gets.

I snort. Yeah right. Jessica doesn't know how to have fun without going full 'Fatal Attraction' on me. I won't be making that mistake again. I take another swig of beer, shaking my head. "Not tonight, Jess." I brush her hand away and move closer to Koa to gain some distance. He's a big guy, taking up most of the couch, but at this point I'd rather be sitting on his knee than have Jessica touch me again. It was partly her fault I was fired. She made such a fuss about guests flirting with me, bringing it to everyone's attention, including the management. When the woman she accused of propositioning me turned out to be related to the captain, I got the blame.

Josh nods towards to door. "Looks like your wish came true."

A rush of adrenaline shoots through my body when Lizzie strolls past. She glances around the room, missing us tucked away in the corner as she heads for the bar.

I stare with a slack-jaw. She's all in white, and under the black light, she resembles an angel on the top of a Christmas tree. Her fluorescent dress clings to her curves and stops just above her knee. Golden bouncy curls fall perfectly around her sweet face and illuminating smile. Everything near the bar is glowing under the black light, but most of all, her.

Jessica turns her head, looking over her shoulder, and furrows her brow. "What are you gawking at?"

I pull my eyebrows together. "Nothing."

She turns her head again and huffs out a laugh. "You're not seriously after Miss Piggy over there?"

"Shut up, Jessica. Why are you always so mean?" I honestly don't know what I ever saw in her other than a talented dancer with a flexible body and she seemed kind and genuine, but I soon learned it was an act. She's a great actor and showgirl, I'll give her that.

"Is she working in the restaurant with you?"

"She's a guest." Koa says. I shoot him a death stare. If he knew Jessica's jealous streak, he wouldn't have said anything.

"I should have known." Jessica sticks out her chin along with her chest as if she could compete with Lizzie. "You never change, Zac. How many millions does this one have? Does she know you're just using her for tips?"

"I'm not using anyone and keep your mouth shut. I

don't want another headache from you or I'll be forced to make a complaint to management." That'll teach her to talk shit about my angel. Wait. What am I saying? She isn't even mine.

Jessica stands up in a huff. "Go fuck yourself." Lifting her head high, she stomps away. Once she's gone, I relax my shoulders a little.

"She was not a happy bunny." Koa chuckles. "What did you do to piss her off?" He brings his drink to his lips.

I shrug my shoulders. "Just one of the many women infatuated with me, I guess."

Koa jabs me playfully on the arm, but it's so hard, I'm sure it's gonna leave a bruise. He doesn't know his own strength. I rub the ache with a chuckle, ignoring his comments about Jessica. I don't want to get into all that now, not when my angel is standing at the bar. Is she looking for me? There's only one way to find out.

CHAPTER
Six

LIZZIE

THERE WERE no free tables in the Italian restaurant tonight, so I ate at the buffet. It was nice, but I missed Zac's annoying flirty banter.

On my way to the room, I bump into Kenna.

"Hey, girlfriend. Where you off to?"

"I was going back for an early night."

"Hell no, you're not. You're coming with me. I'm going to sneak into the crew bar for the inside gossip on crew life."

My pulse quickens at the thought of seeing Zac. "Can you sneak me in too?"

"Absolutely. Are you ready to go? I'm on my way there now."

"Let's go."

The opulence of the ship fades as we descend into the bowel of the boat, through a staff only door. Chipped paint flakes from the metal bannister as I walk down the stairs with stark walls, getting more depressing the further we delve. We slink into a dimly lit room with wood panelling lining the wall. Weaving in and out of the tables, I scan the room for Zac, but I can't see in the dark crevices.

We approach the bar at the far end with a black light

above, and I'm almost blinded by the bartender's fluorescent teeth. The whites of his eyes pop too, and it makes me giggle.

"What's funny?" Kenna asks.

I whisper, "His teeth are so bright."

She laughs. "So are yours, honey."

I cover my mouth, suddenly self-conscious of looking a prat under this lighting.

"What can I get you?" the bartender asks.

Kenna asks for a cocktail.

"Hmm, I'll have a..." My drink of choice is a wine, but it's out-of-place down here and we need to blend in. Thinking of blending in, I should have changed into something casual, instead of standing out in a bright white dress like a giant marshmallow. My breath hitches. I'm in white. Heat prickles my skin as I look down at myself, glowing under the black light. "Can I have half a pint of cider, please?" I need to get away from this illuminating bar, and fast.

Kenna hands some cash over. I turn around and bump into a solid chest. My eyes follow the white shirt and buttons upwards, all the way to the collar, over the scruff on his jaw and around his beautiful mouth and scar above his lip. The whites of his eyes surrounding those vibrant green irises are brighter than the brightest star. "Zac," I whisper, barely audible over the music.

"How did you get down here?"

I look at Kenna and shrug my shoulders.

"Come and sit with us." He takes my hand, and the feel of his palm in mine sends a ripple of goosebumps up my arm, forcing the hairs on my skin to perk up. I glance at Kenna and wave for her to follow. I'm not the sort of girl that ditches her friend at the first sight of a man.

Zac gestures to another guy to move, and I sit next to Zac on a padded two-seater sofa. The lights are low in this little nook and I'm thankful I'm no longer luminous.

The big guy makes space for Kenna between him and Zac's waiter friend at the opposite end of the table and she's her usual chatty self, gathering all the information she requires for her work.

Zac moves closer, creaking the leather as he places his arm over the back of the sofa. He buries his face in my neck, brushing his lips against my skin. My muscles tense, and I freeze.

"Relax, it's just me," he whispers in my ear. His hand glides up my thigh, making my heart race and my breasts rise and fall with my erratic breathing.

"It's kind of hard to relax when you rub my leg like that." I glance down at his hand and back to his eyes. The thumping in my chest drowns out the music in my ears.

"Do you want me to stop?"

I bite my lip hard. I don't want him to stop, but I can't think straight with him touching me like that. My head nods, but my mind is willing his fingers higher to my apex.

He removes his hand, taking a sip of his pint and I relax my shoulders, letting out a sigh of relief. Or is it disappointment? The sudden loss of contact leaves me with an ache deep in my centre.

Placing his pint back on the table, he bumps my shoulder with a smile. "So how old are you?"

I curl my lips. "How old do you think I am?"

He shrugs. "In your thirties"

"Wow, you really know how to make a girl feel good."

"Why are you forty?" His cocky grin spreads across his face.

I can't tell if he's joking or being serious. "Judging by your maturity, you must be nineteen."

He chuckles. "Would it bother you if I were?"

I cock an eyebrow. "You're not that young." Is he? I was only kidding. "Would it bother you if I was forty?"

"I like older women."

I sip my cider, wetting my dry lips and quenching my parched throat. "Too bad I'm only thirty then."

"So I was right the first time." His shoulder bumps mine.

"No, you said I was in my thirties. I'm not *in*. I've barely just arrived."

"You're still older than me, Mrs Robinson."

I roll my eyes. "That's so overused. And besides, I'm not married, and I haven't done anything with you."

"Yet."

He's so cocky. It annoys me. "Okay, so tell me, Benjamin. How old are you?"

"It's Zac. You forgot my name already?"

"Benjamin from the film. You can't be that young or you wouldn't be referencing 'The Graduate'."

"I'm not so old I know what film Mrs Robinson is from or the other characters' names."

"Oh please. Neither am I. I just like old movies. I'm not a cougar. I'm a kitten."

"Is that so?"

I giggle. "Come on. Just tell me how old you are."

"I'm twenty-five."

"That's not even an age gap." I swat his chest and he chuckles.

"Oh, I have something for you." He pulls his wallet from his trousers and opens it up.

I hold my hand up. "Please, you're not giving me a condom, are you?"

He looks up with an eyebrow raised and a curl forming in the corner of his mouth. "No, but I can if you want."

I lean closer to get a peek and see my shiny necklace with the topaz jewel droplet. "You found it?" My hands cover my mouth and tears threaten my eyes.

"Yeah, I went to the pool to look for it and someone had handed it in to the lifeguards. The hoop to your clasp had opened up slightly, but I fixed it."

"Thank you so much. You've no idea what that means to me. Will you put it on for me?" I turn my back to him and move my hair out of the way.

His hot breath lands on my bare skin at the back of my neck, sending a cascade of tingles down my spine

He breathes me in again. "You smell so good." His fingers graze my collarbone as he places the necklace around me. "Have I earned some brownie points?"

My body vibrates with every graze of his hand and each whisper from his lips. "Zac, you've earned the entire cake. Thank you."

He turns me around and twists the jewel the right way. "There." His fingers linger on my chest before sliding down the curve of my breast. His tongue darts out to wet his lips, and he reaches for his pint.

With a shaky hand, he knocks the glass, and it topples

over in slow motion. He moves his other hand to snatch the pot, but it's too late. The cool beer flies through the air, landing in my cleavage, and the rest goes to my lap, seeping into the fabric of my dress as though I've wet myself. The beer smell hits me, like I've just stepped into a brewery.

"Fuck, sorry." Zac picks up the empty pint pot, whips off his waistcoat and hands it to me.

"What am I supposed to do with this?" I use it as a mop to soak up the spillage.

Zac nods to my breasts. "Cover yourself."

I glance down at my white dress, now opaque, showing my white lace bra. Gasping, I pull the waistcoat to my chest and stare at my thighs, now visible through the fabric. My eyes plead with Kenna for help, who throws some tissues at me from her bag.

Zac stands, taking my hand and I follow his lead, clutching the waistcoat close to my body to hide the stain and keep my modesty. We walk down a narrow corridor, stopping as he pulls me into a small cabin. He closes the door behind me and we stand close together in the small walkway between the bathroom and a closet.

I hand him his waistcoat back. "Do you have a wet flannel or something? I need to wipe this off my chest."

He smirks. "I can lick it off for you if you like."

I giggle, but swat his arm. My chest heaves, making me aware of my panting breaths.

Zac throws his dirty waistcoat in a bag in the bathroom. "Take your dress off."

I stand wide-eyed, staring at him with my mouth open. He hasn't even kissed me yet, and he's already demanding

I strip. "No. Pervert. You spilled that drink on purpose, didn't you? Thinking you can get me back to your room, and I'll just bend over for you."

He grabs a white cruise line robe. "I only wanted to take it to the laundrette. Sasha will wash it for you so it doesn't stain. But I'm liking what you said more. If you want to bend over, be my guest."

A smirk is fixed on his annoyingly perfect face, and I want to kiss it off. Stop. Stop. Stop. I give my head a shake, trying to get the image of snogging his face out of my mind.

He holds the robe out in front of him and nods to the bathroom. "If I carry on staring at your nipples through that dress, I'll be bending you over this desk."

"Ugh." I snatch the robe and step into the tiny bathroom, if you can call it that. It's so cramped. I could literally sit on the toilet, shower, and wash my hands at the same time. After peeling the dress from my skin, I wet the corner of a towel to wipe away the sticky coating and wrap the robe around me. It only just meets, so I tie it tight, not taking any chances of him seeing me in my underwear, even though he's no doubt had a good look already.

My knickers are damp from the beer…and other things, and are slightly see-through, reminding me I haven't waxed down there in a long time. Perhaps I should visit the salon. No. Nothing is going to happen between us and besides, I'm not waxing for a man. I step back out into the room and hand Zac my dress.

"Back in a minute." He leaves me alone to explore his cabin. The bottom bunk bed is perfectly made and the top one is messy, with a Hogwarts t-shirt hanging from the rail. A laptop sits on a small desk with a Harry Potter sticker on it, and I wonder if he's a fan or his roommate.

My hand moves over an array of toiletries lining the chest of drawers—mostly expensive aftershave—no wonder he always smells so good. He must earn a good whack to afford these. A photo pinned on the wall catches my eye; Zac with his arm draped over an older woman. He wasn't kidding when he said he likes older women.

Zac bursts back into the room with laboured breath, as if he's sprinted there and back. "Sasha will clean your dress. She says it will be ready in the morning. I'll ask Koa to bring it to your cabin when he does the morning rounds."

"Thank you."

"Now where were we? Oh yeah, you were going to bend over." He cocks an eyebrow and smiles as he steps closer.

I giggle. "I don't bend over for any man."

"Lie down then. I'm not fussy."

I swat his chest. "You're insufferable."

"I want my cake. You said I'd earned it." He grins, then laughs when I roll my eyes but stand with my arms folded across my chest, tapping my foot. If I don't remove myself from this situation soon, I will be in his bed doubled over or however he wants to take me.

"I bet you're one of those too, aren't you?"

His eyebrows pinch. "One of what?"

"A Slytherin." I scowl.

He gasps, placing his hand on his chest. "I'm hurt. How dare you? I'm a Hufflepuff."

I flinch my head back. "Really?"

"Yeah. I'm loyal and hardworking. Let me guess, miss bossy-boots, you must be Gryffindor."

"Nope. Wrong again. I'm Hufflepuff."

"Ah yes, I remember the loyal swallow tat." He closes the gap between us. "Now, what can I spill on this robe to get you naked?"

"You could just ask me to take it off."

He raises an eyebrow, making the thin silvery scar more visible on his temple. It looks like it was a nasty cut and I want to kiss it better, but I resist the urge.

"It won't get you very far, mind."

He tugs at the tie around my waist. "My kitten, always toying with me."

I push him back slightly, giggling, and look away. Any minute now, I will plant my lips on his mouth if he continues teasing me. "Which bed's yours, anyway?"

"You wanna sleep over?"

"No. I'm just curious."

"The top."

"There's no headspace up there."

He tugs at the tie around my waist again, pulling me to him so our bodies collide. His warm breath rests on my cheek. "You won't need headspace when you're on your back."

My body stills. I think my breathing has stopped along with my heart. The tie on my robe loosens and a rough hand slips between the opening and touches the bare skin of my pillowy stomach. With a tremble, his palm glides along my waist to my back, and I sense the nerves underneath his cocky exterior.

Sparks fire off in all directions with each stroke of his fingers against my bare skin, and I'm lost in the forest again as I gaze into his eyes. Mesmerised by his touch, his words. Him. His other hand caresses my cheek, tangling his fingers in my curls, and I part my mouth, awaiting his kiss.

The door swings open, breaking my trance. I draw in a breath and crook my neck to see the big guy standing in the doorway, taking us in. "Sorry, am I interrupting something?"

Zac takes hold of my robe and pulls it together, tying the strap. I hadn't realised it had fallen open. Gosh, the embarrassment. It's bad enough that Zac has seen me like that, but his roommate.

My cheeks burn hotter than the sun. "It's okay. I was just leaving." Stepping away from Zac, I dash to the exit, ducking under the guy's arm as he leans against the doorjamb. I can't get out fast enough.

With swift feet, I almost break into a sprint. A flush creeps up my neck, and I pull my robe together, making sure it's covering me.

"Lizzie, wait up," Zac shouts. He runs and catches up with me just as I step into the lift to take me to my deck.

"Goodnight, Zac." The doors close before he can stop them and the lift ascends.

CHAPTER
Seven

ZAC

I DIDN'T CHASE her last night after getting the impression she was glad that Koa interrupted us. I think I was too. Our first kiss is going to be special, not a quick grope in my crappy cabin. I don't know where yet, but I'm going to kiss her before her trip is over.

I know I shouldn't be getting involved with guests. I've never brought one back to the room before, and I've certainly never kissed one before. If I had kissed her last night, I wouldn't have been able to stop. Ten minutes later and Koa may have walked into an x-rated scene.

Because I have to work today, I write a note asking her to meet me at the buffet dining room at six. I finish work with enough time to shower and dress for the evening. I want to get to know her more over dinner. We can have a few drinks in the bar, then I'll sneak that kiss.

The boat sways under my feet. There's a storm on the horizon tonight. I step out of the shower and dress in dark jeans and a blue shirt. I want to look smart, but casual. She always sees me in my uniform.

As I walk to the restaurant, the floor shifts under my feet. I glance through the round windows on the doors to the deck and see the dark clouds rolling in and a light rain hit the glass. I grab hold of the railing as the ship tilts again. Fuck, this isn't good. The area to the pool is closed, and all doors leading to the promenade are sectioned off.

I wait just outside the restaurant where I asked her to meet me and see a queue forming. They're busy tonight. It looks like the entire ship's guest list has decided to eat at the same time. There's not much else to do though, seeing as everything outside is closed because of the storm.

Thirty minutes go by. She hasn't turned up. I check my watch again, wondering if she saw the message. Has she gone to the other restaurant? I make my way down to the Italian to check she's there. The floor sways, and I grip the railing as I walk down the steps. They're swamped too. I've never seen it so busy.

"Josh, have you seen Lizzie?"

"Who?"

"The curly blonde."

"Big tits, cute, curvy hips?"

I snarl at Josh and clench my jaw, but haven't time to argue with him. "Yes. Have you seen her tonight?"

"No. Have you checked the bookings? If she hasn't booked in, she won't be getting a seat."

I check the sheet and don't see her name.

The manager pats me on the back. "Zac, get changed and give us a hand. I need all hands on deck tonight."

"I have the night off. I've been working all day."

"I'll give you time off when we stop at one of the ports. It's packed solid tonight."

I huff and stomp in the back to where some spare uniforms are kept. Changing, all I can think about is Lizzie and why she didn't show. Is she mad at me? I'm sure she got the note. Koa said he delivered it personally, along with the dress.

Once the restaurant quiets down, I change back into my casual clothes and jog to the lift, making my way to her room, desperate to check on her. I knock on the door, but there's no answer. My fist pounds louder this time. "Lizzie, are you there?"

"Go away," she shouts.

Fuck, she is mad. What have I done? "Elizabeth, talk to me. What's wrong?"

"Go away, please."

"I'm not going anywhere until you talk to me. Was it last night? If I came on too strong, I apologise. We can just be friends." If friendship's all she wants. I'll take it.

"It's fine. I don't want to be friends."

My mind scrambles to think where it all went wrong. "What have I done to upset you?"

"You haven't upset me."

The ship tilts again like it has been all night. I hold on to the door handle. "Open the door, then."

"I'll see you tomorrow. I'm in bed."

Is she with someone? Fuck, it hadn't crossed my mind that she could have someone in bed with her.

There's a bang and a crash. "Are you all right?"

"I'm fine. Everything is fine. Please, Zac."

"Elizabeth, I can tell from your voice something's wrong. Just open the door, please."

The toilet flushes, then the handle pulls down. The door creaks as it opens a fraction.

"Don't look at me. I'm sick."

I push the door open, forcing her to step aside. Relief

pulses through me. I'm not glad she's sick, but I am glad she's alone.

"What's wrong? Is it something you've eaten?"

She shakes her head. "I haven't eaten anything since lunch. I think I'm seasick."

"Have you taken anything?"

"Only some Dramamine, but it's not helped much. Just made me drowsy."

"I know it's probably the last thing you want, but you should eat. It helps. Let me get you some food."

"I can't stomach a meal, Zac. I'll just throw it up again."

"I'll get you something to help you feel better. You might want to take a shower, too."

Horror floods her eyes, and she covers her face. "Do I look that bad?"

"No sweetheart, but you have puke in your hair. I'll be back in fifteen."

I make my way to the restaurant and rustle her up some food.

When I return, she's showered and washed her hair, wearing shorts and a mermaid t-shirt that says 'Mermaids don't have thigh gaps'. It makes me chuckle. "Nice tee."

"I know you're not looking at the tee." She's right. I couldn't help notice her tits or her erect nipples under her tee. They jiggle more than usual when she walks to the bed, confirming she's braless.

I place the tray on the dressing table. "Here, I got you some toast. The lemon tea and ginger cookies will help with the nausea."

"Thank you." She nibbles at the toast, taking small

delicate bites. My pockets are full of more lemon tea sachets I took from the restaurant and some ginger and peppermint tea bags, too, and I place them on her hospitality tray.

I sit down in the chair at her dressing table. "Can I get you anything else?"

She shakes her head. "I'm sorry I didn't meet you. I really wanted to, but I fell asleep after being sick, and I've just felt awful for the rest of the evening."

"Don't worry about it. Another time."

LIZZIE

HEAVY RAIN BEATS down on the veranda, hitting the sliding door. Zac opens it a little more, allowing fresh air to circulate around the room, which helps to remove the sickly smell of the cabin.

I sip my tea and pop another Dramamine. "Will you sit with me for a while?"

"If you want me to." The bed dips when Zac slides next to me. He moves the wet hair from my face. "Has the toast helped?"

"A little. I think you talking to me and taking my mind off it has helped more." I keep sipping my tea and munch on a ginger biscuit. It's so weird how he calls a ginger nut a cookie.

Zac picks up my Cosmo magazine from the nightstand.

I brush the biscuit crumbs from my breasts. "You love

that magazine, don't you? I'll get you a yearly subscription for your birthday."

"At least you're smiling again." He winks, sending a flutter to my centre.

I take another sip of tea, washing down the biscuit. "When is your birthday, anyway?"

"November 11ᵗʰ. When's yours?"

"July 31ˢᵗ."

He flicks to the back of the magazine. "So you're a Leo. You are a cougar."

I swat his chest. "I told you, I'm a kitten. Stop teasing me. I'm ill."

He grins, then reads aloud. "The Sun is entering Scorpio on Saturday. After that, your life will pick up the pace—especially when it comes to life in the bedroom. If you're single and looking to fool around, this astro-weather really supports hooking up and flirting. Put yourself out there, kitten. And if you're looking for a hot waiter, he won't disappoint you."

I giggle. "It does not say that."

"It does."

I snatch the magazine from him. Smiling as I read it.

"See. I just added the bit about the hot waiter. I don't need the stars to predict the future with us."

I raise an eyebrow. "You really are too cocky for your own good. And I'm too ill to be having this conversation."

He leans back against the headboard, adjusting the pillow to make himself comfy. The wind howls through the gap in the patio door, sending in a nice welcoming fresh breeze from the cold night air.

"11ᵗʰ November did you say?"

"Yep."

I search the list of star signs until I reach that date. "You're a Scorpio. The stars are urging you to shake up your love life."

"I'm trying." He chuckles.

I continue to read his horoscope. "If you see someone you're interested in trying out, just go for it. Don't overthink things, just keep your eye on the prize."

"Does it really say that, or are you giving me the green light?"

"Er, I'm nobody's prize, and you're not trying me out. Thank you."

He takes the magazine from me and finishes the paragraph. "Something that starts out as a flirtationship could become a significant relationship later on." He wiggles his eyebrows.

"Like that's really going to happen." I yawn, placing my empty mug on the nightstand.

He rubs my back. "Has the Dramamine kicked in?"

I lay down and close my eyes. "Will you stay?"

"Sure. Get some sleep, the storm will pass, and you'll feel better in the morning. Then we can fuck."

I slap his thigh.

"Feisty. My kinda woman."

"Zac, stop. Shut up and read your magazine."

"Okay, I'll just sit here and read about sex sessions that ended in the ER."

"Thank you for staying."

He leans over and kisses my cheek. His warm lips send tingles rippling across my face.

"I have something for you in the bedside cabinet drawer."

"It's fine, I have my own johnny's."

I tut and roll my eyes. "Just open the drawer."

He pulls out the chocolate mint coins, wrapped in shiny green foil that appear on my pillow each night. "What's this for?"

"Your tip." I giggle. "I get one every night on my pillow and I don't even like mint."

He shrugs. "Best tip I ever got." He peels the wrapper from one and pops it in his mouth, then picks the magazine up again. Settling back on the bed, he strokes my forehead with his fingers, brushing the damp hair from my face. "Night kitten."

CHAPTER Eight

LIZZIE

THE SUN POURS through the balcony doors, blinding my eyes. I roll over onto the next pillow and my forehead sticks to a piece of crisp paper. I peel it from me and blink as I read the note.

Morning kitten.
I had to split to change for the breakfast shift. Enjoy your day in Honolulu. Catch up with you later.
PS. You have a cute purr when you sleep.

I smile at the last line. My skin is tight where a dry patch of drool flakes off near my mouth. A wave of dread crashes against my chest, and my heart sinks. Oh my goodness, he saw me like this. How loud was I snoring? Did he stay here all night? Then I remember last night and how he saw me much worse with sick in my hair. Ew. A shudder vibrates within me and I shake the thought away.

Still holding the note, I jump from the bed and walk to the balcony, inhaling the morning breeze. The cityscape of

Honolulu stands proud, and I can't wait to explore. I also need a Hawaiian outfit for the themed dinner this evening. Something sexy for Zac to notice me. Although I'm not sure it's necessary, he seems to like whatever I wear, even my mermaid pj's.

After dressing, I make my way to the buffet breakfast, hoping I will see Zac.

Walking past the casino, everything is quiet and not the usual hive of activity from the previous days. I wish I'd played on the machines when I had the chance. Hopefully, they'll come alive again on the trip back to LA. The shops are still open though and I make a mental note to buy a few bottles of perfume while I'm here and pick up some gifts for Eddie, Susie and my niece, Rosie.

I head over to the cooked breakfast behind the buffet counter. Zac stops serving when he spots me in the queue, and his smile reaches his eyes.

When I get closer to his station, I lean over the counter and whisper, "Thank you for last night."

"No worries. I kinda want you to be sick every night so I can cuddle you."

The heat rises to my cheeks, and I look away. Turning back to him, I say, "You can cuddle me anytime, not just when I'm sick."

"I'll take you up on that."

"What time do you finish? I can wait for you, and we can go into Honolulu together."

"I'd love that, but I'm working this afternoon, too. We're getting everything ready for the themed dinner."

"Oh, I guess I'll see you later, then."

"Yeah, don't you worry. I'll definitely be seeing you later."

There's a flutter in my stomach as if a school of fish are trapped in a tank, swimming in every direction.

ZAC

I'LL BE happy when this day ends. My body aches from helping with the restaurant decorations, and I'm tired. I got little sleep last night in her bed. I spent half the night watching her sleep and the other half with a boner.

When she rolled over in her sleep and snuggled into me, her hand fell onto my chest, and I held it in mine, thinking about spending my nights with her. I've never felt like this about anyone before, not after a week anyway, but there's a vulnerability in her, making me want to take care of her. Even though I have nothing to offer. I don't even have a fixed address, but a woman like her doesn't need a younger man to take care of her. I know she's independent with her own money. Maybe I could be there to talk about her day, bring her tea when she's unwell, run her a bath when she's tired, and take care of her like a man takes care of his woman.

As the guests clamber into the Hawaiian themed dinner, I walk to a table with a tray of drinks, and those red patent shoes come into view.

My eyes rake the soft skin of her legs past her knee where her floral dress flaps open as she walks. Her beautiful smile lights up the room even when she's not under a black light.

My breath catches in my throat. I stop in my tracks, taking in every inch of her. She sees me and smiles, mouthing the word hi as she waves. I balance the tray with one hand and wave back at her.

The tray slips. Time slows down as the drinks topple, and wetness seeps through the fabric of my shirt and slacks. Fuck, why do I keep doing that? I catch the glasses with my free hand and set them straight on the tray before they tumble to the floor, but I'm now wearing the contents. I glance back over at her, giggling as Josh shows her to a table.

Sally comes over and takes the tray from me. "Go clean yourself up. I got this." She retreats behind the bar to get fresh drinks for the guests while I head into the back and borrow some spare clothes. How can she have such an effect on me? She must think I'm one clumsy fool.

The staff room is empty, and I quickly whip off my wet pants, vest, and shirt. I pull out a clean set of clothes from a hanger in the closet that we keep for emergencies. As I turn around, shrugging the shirt on, my eyes widen, taking her in before me. "You shouldn't be in here."

She steps closer, her gaze moves from my chest to my face. "I know, but I wanted to see you." She takes the hem of my shirt in her hands and buttons it up. "I haven't stopped thinking about you all day."

"Me neither. Did you have fun in Honolulu?"

She nods and bites her lip as she continues to button my shirt.

"If you're caught in here, I could get fired."

"Oh, sorry. I didn't think. I'll go." She turns, but I catch her wrist and pull her back to me, placing her hand on my pounding chest.

"Don't go."

She takes quick panting breaths and parts her lips. My fingers graze her cheek. My mouth inches closer to hers and she dips her head back slightly, closing her eyes, ready for me to take what I want.

"Hurry up, dickhead. We're slammed out here." Josh shouts, swinging the door open.

Lizzie freezes, blinking rapidly. Josh stares at us. My jaw tenses as I glare back at Josh. I'm thankful it was him and not the manager, but damn—will I ever get a chance to kiss this woman?

"I'm sorry. I'll see you later?" Her eyes plead with me.

"You can count on it."

She disappears as I pull on clean slacks.

"Bro, you're seriously pushing your luck. What were you doing? What if I was someone else?"

"I didn't tell her to come in here. She just showed up."

"You weren't exactly fighting her off. Look if you're doing this to prove a point. You win. I get it. She's into you. No need to make waves."

"I'm not trying to prove a point. I actually like her. And do you honestly think she's into me?"

"Argh, dude. You're sailing close to the wind with this one." He flies out the door as quick as he came in, leaving me to finish changing into the clean uniform.

As the night progresses, I can't keep my eyes off her. She's sitting with a group of others, chatting away and looking beautiful, especially when she laughs. Now and then, I catch her eye. I wish I was waiting on her tonight, but I couldn't switch.

After the meal, the guests at her table leave her sitting there alone. She runs a finger around the rim of her wineglass while watching me clear away plates.

I meander around the tables, making my way to her. "Are you waiting for me?"

"Is that all right?"

"Yeah, but you might have a long wait. I don't finish until late. I have to help take the decorations down and get the restaurant ready for breakfast in the morning."

"Oh. I guess I'll see you tomorrow then?"

"Yeah. Did you enjoy the food tonight?"

"Those little mini Hawaiian desserts were delish, but I only had three." She pouts her lower lip, making me want to take it between my teeth.

"I'll see if we have any more."

She yawns. "I think I'll just go back to the room and relax."

"I'll stop by if I get any room service orders your way."

"I'd like that."

"Maybe I'll get to see you in your pyjamas again."

She giggles. "Zac."

"Or maybe a robe with nothing underneath." I add, wanting to see her blush again.

Her eyes flick to the ceiling, but she has a hint of a smile as her lip twitches. "Dream on."

Nothing would feel more right than to kiss her nose, cheeks, lips and say goodnight. I'm almost afraid to make a move after earlier. If I'm caught, I'll be kicked off this ship at the next port, but I can't resist her. I want her. No, want isn't the right word. I need her like a junkie needs their next fix. I'm getting addicted to her and how she makes me feel, but I wouldn't have it any other way.

CHAPTER Nine

LIZZIE

AFTER TAKING a leisurely walk around the promenade deck, I arrive back at my cabin. My bed's turned down for the night with a little chocolate on my pillow, in an orange wrapper this time. Chocolate orange. I smile, knowing Zac had something to do with this.

A bundle of fresh towels has appeared at the foot of the bed with the top one in the shape of a swan. I love these little touches. Slipping out of my heels, I wiggle my toes. Even though I've been sitting most of the night, my feet aren't used to fancy footwear.

I change into something more comfortable, open the sliding balcony doors and step outside into the cool night air. The gentle breeze swathes my skin as I look out at the calm sea, listening to the soft hum of the engine and water lapping against the hull.

My mind wanders to Zac and my heart swells like the waves before me. I really like him, but I'm afraid of getting hurt again. A knock at the door disturbs my musings and, with bare feet, I pad through the room. Excitement bubbles at the thought of seeing Zac again.

My mouth drops open at the stack of mini desserts

piled high on a plate in a pyramid shape. Peering behind it is his gorgeous smile. "Zac?"

"Is this better for you?"

"Wow, yes, it looks amazing. Come in." I stand to the side, propping the door open, allowing Zac to step through, holding the plate with one large hand underneath. He drops it onto the dressing table and turns to look me up and down. His eyes rest on my breasts, and he chuckles.

I draw in a breath and look down at the slogan on my tee. 'Big girls do it better.' From one of my body positivity kicks that I was on last summer.

"Is that so?" He points at my chest.

"I'll let you be the judge of that."

"Will you now?" His deep voice vibrates through my body. "And what exactly is it that you do better?"

A smile spreads across my flushed face. "Cuddle, of course."

He chuckles again. I reach behind him to pinch a mini Hawaiian dream cake, but he catches my hand and pulls me close, acting as a barrier between me and the cakes. "There's something sweeter than those desserts."

Stepping back out of his grasp, I place my hands on my hips. "And what would that be?"

He taps his lips and quirks a grin. "A kiss."

To stifle my laugh, I chew on the inside of my mouth. "I'd sooner have a cake." As much as I want to kiss him, I don't know if I should. I always let my heart be my compass, but right now I'm sinking.

"You want to kiss me. You were desperate to kiss me in the staff room earlier."

Who does this guy think he is, Zac Efron? He's right, of course, but I'm not making his head bigger than it already is.

"No, I wasn't. I don't want to kiss anyone. I hate all men, remember?"

A strange noise coming from outside piques my interest and we both glance towards the balcony. I step through the curtain into the cool breeze.

Zac follows. "You said you make exceptions for waiters."

"Did I?" I glance around, wondering where the noises are coming from.

He steps closer. "I'm pretty sure you did."

"Hush, let me listen."

There's a moan coming from the balcony above and a grunt. My eyes bulge at Zac. His chest shakes, shuddering with a silent laugh.

"Are they?" My mouth parts.

More moans and noises. "Daddy."

I mouth the words 'Oh my gosh'. Pointing to the balcony above, I whisper, "Did she just call him daddy?"

Zac closes the gap between us. "You like to listen, huh?"

I put my hand over his mouth. "Shh."

The moans are louder, along with a rhythmic slapping of flesh on flesh. I'm not sure who's up there, but they sound like they're having a great time.

Zac presses his lips against the palm of my hand and then nips my fingers. He pushes me back against the railing and I remove my hand from his mouth to grip the metal bar.

"This is turning you on, isn't it?"

"Don't be ridiculous."

His chest presses against my breasts, forcing me to lean back and hold on tighter to the railing. A finger hooks over the elastic to my pyjama shorts, and I draw in a breath.

"Zac."

His other hand wraps around my throat, then he brings his thumb over my lips, keeping his fingers curled around my neck. "Shh, princess."

I glance around at the adjoining balconies to check we're alone.

His hand trails down further inside my shorts. "No panties," he whispers, then curls his lip upwards in the corner.

More moans rain down from above, and I let out a moan of my own as a finger slips between my folds, circling my bundle of nerves.

"You sure are wet, sweetheart, to say you're not turned on."

I flare my nostrils and slant my eyes, but then close them because I don't want him to stop, even though his smugness annoys me.

He dips a finger inside then rubs more circles around, lathering me up in the slickness. My hips rock uncontrollably, and my hums and moans become louder.

His thumb strokes my neck. "Open your eyes."

I can't seem to open them. I'm swept away at sea with nothing but his fingers pleasuring me and his hot breath on my mouth.

"Open your eyes, Lizzie," he growls. "I want you to see who's making you come."

I gasp and my eyes flick wide open, staring at his gorgeous face. He sees the real me, and I'm vulnerable, scared, and wish I'd got that wax now. But he doesn't seem to mind and continues to pleasure me. His fingers flicker deep inside while his thumb applies the right amount of pressure to my throbbing bud.

His hot breath pants onto my mouth. He's so close. Kiss me, just kiss me, please. My hands still grip the railing, unable to let go in fear I'll collapse into a pool on the balcony floor.

His hand loosens around my neck and clutches the curls at the back of my head. He pulls down on my hair, forcing my head back, allowing him to delicately suck on my neck.

My eyes dart to the sky, and my breath quickens. The stars twinkle above me in the clear night sky. The Big Dipper stands out, and I feel like I'm on the Big Dipper ride at Blackpool Pleasure Beach. My stomach flips with every stroke of his tongue and my core pulses with every flick of his fingers. The heat between us is scorching like the sun and even though the cool night air blows through my curls, my body temperature rises.

"Zac." His name leaves my lips as a breathy whisper, and I pant out in quick bursts.

"Yes, kitten."

"Oh gosh, don't stop."

His erection grinds into my hips, and still gripping my hair, he forces my head forward to look into his eyes. "I'm not stopping."

My eyes flicker and close.

"I told you to look at me when you come." His voice is

deep and commanding, like he's straining. Opening my eyes to obey, I'm pulled into depths as dark and deadly as a tropical rainforest.

He holds my head in place while his other hand works its magic. Another circle of his thumb, a flicker of his fingers, and I come undone. My walls clamp down around him, throbbing and clenching his fingers. My breath comes out in short sharp bursts, and my eyes don't leave his gaze as his fingers slow their rhythm. The grip on my hair loosens, and he watches me with hooded eyes as I come down from my ride.

"Breathtaking," he says with his mouth still open, but so close to mine I can breathe in his air. Is he talking about me or the scenery? Whatever he's referring to, he's the one that took my breath away.

"It really was," I whisper, aware we're still on the balcony. The moans from above come back into earshot. They had faded a moment ago when all I could hear was the lapping of the ocean and the pulse of Zac's heart along with his ragged breaths. He still has his hand down my shorts, cupping between my thighs. I release my hold on the metal railing and move my hand to undo his belt and return the favour. He whips his hand from my shorts and grabs my wrist before I can feel his erection in my hand.

"Not now. I have to get back to work."

He pecks my nose and walks back into the room, picking up a mini cake from the dressing table and placing it in his mouth in one bite. My legs are like jelly. I'm still panting as I wobble back into the room. He picks up another cake and winks as he opens the door.

"Aren't you going to at least wash your hands?"

He chuckles, then brings two fingers to his mouth and sucks them clean. "Sleep well, kitten." He closes the door behind him, leaving me with weak knees and a delirious smile on my face.

I flop on the bed, staring at the ceiling. I need to book in at the salon tomorrow. If anything happens again, I don't want him to see me unkempt. No. I won't change myself for a man. But I also want his fingers there again and more, his mouth. How he sucked on my neck, I imagine him sucking elsewhere.

My fingers graze my skin where his lips trailed, and I relive the sensation of his mouth like hot syrup enveloping my flesh. I wanted to feel his tongue in my mouth and his warm lips pressed against mine.

Why didn't he kiss me? Is it because I refused him initially? He should know I was only teasing. He seems to get me. I worry he sees the real me sometimes when I feel him boring into my soul. But if he knew the real me, would he still hang around?

AFTER THE FORMAL dinner for the Valentine's Masquerade ball, I hover in the bar, sipping a 'Love Potion' cocktail. Two hands squeeze my bottom through the red silky fabric of my gown. I draw in a breath, inhaling his familiar scent of pine trees with a hint of lemon. The hairs prickle on my skin when the scruff of his jaw brushes my neck, and a glorious tingle shoots down my spine, causing me to shiver in delight.

"It's only me," he whispers before trailing kisses down my neck, and hugging my waist from behind.

I smile. "How did you know it was me?"

A puff of air escapes his lips. "I'd know this ass anywhere."

I turn around to face him, and peer into eyes darker behind an ebony mask edged in gold. "Are you saying I have a big arse?" I know I do, but I don't need him to point it out to me.

He smiles, moving his hands back to my plump cheeks. "I'm saying you have the most perfect ass I've ever seen." He leans into my ear again. "An ass I can't wait to bury my cock inside later."

I gasp with wide eyes, then swallow. "You're so confident, aren't you?"

He winks, causing a flicker in my centre and I purse my lips to stop a smile spreading on my face. There's no way he's fucking my arse, but I want those succulent lips on me again. My eyes wander down his body, checking out the tux he's sporting. The black bowtie sits perfectly under the collar of his white dinner shirt and the black jacket looks a little big, but he pulls it off so well.

"Aren't you supposed to be working?"

"I called in sick." He places a finger in front of his lips. "Shh."

My eyebrows squish together. "How come?"

"I couldn't have Cinderella going to the ball alone, could I?" If he only knew how much of that statement is true. I really do feel like Cinderella, trying to fit in and be someone I'm not.

With excitement coursing through my veins, I place my

hands on his shoulders. "I'm so glad you're here. I was disappointed when I didn't see you during dinner."

My feathered, sequined mask clashes with his rigid one as we hug.

"I'm here now. I couldn't risk being seen by my manager during dinner. Plus, I was in the laundrette, trying to find a suit that fit."

My head flinches back. "Isn't this yours?"

"I'm borrowing it. Shh." He delicately pecks my nose. "Have you seen the chocolate fountain?"

"No." I look around the room for said fountain. The word chocolate exciting me as much as him.

"Over here." He takes my hand and leads me through a flock of people to the other side of the ballroom. An array of strawberries, marshmallows, kiwi, pineapple, and other fruit and nibbles surround a huge fountain of chocolate in the middle of a round table.

"Wow, Zac. I've never seen one this big."

He looks down at his dick. "Thanks for the compliment, sweetheart."

I giggle and swat his chest, then take a stick with skewered strawberries and run it under the cascade of melted chocolate. The rich cocoa wafts all around me, causing my tastebuds to prick up in anticipation.

Bringing it to my lips, the chocolate drips on my breasts. A red blush breaks out on my chest, sending the heat up my neck to paint my cheeks.

Zac wipes the drips with his finger and licks the pad before biting into a strawberry from the stick I had forgotten I was holding. Another drip drops down my cleavage. My eyes look down and then back to his face.

"Don't worry about that. I'll lick that off later."

"Oh, will you?" I pant the words, hoping he'll follow through with his promise.

"Come and dance with me." He nods to the dimly lit dance floor. The long red velvet curtains frame the windows, and the tall candelabras give off a perfect glow.

I shake my head. "I'm not much of a dancer."

He chuckles. "It's slow dancing. We're not doing the Macarena."

Bruno Mars, 'Just The Way You Are' plays. Zac smiles, holds my hand and pulls me to the dance floor. We weave in and out of the crowd until we find an empty spot in the middle, kicking aside the heart-shaped balloons scattered around.

He lifts my arms over his shoulders, and I clasp my hands around his neck. Gazing into his eyes makes my stomach pop like a bottle of champagne overflowing with fizz. His hands move to my arse and squeeze my cheeks, forcing our bodies flush.

I draw in a breath as his erection presses into my hip. "You said this was slow dancing, not dirty dancing."

He moves my hair from my ear and whispers, "I can't help it. You always have this effect on me."

"That and spilling drinks?"

"That as well." Our noses touch. He's so close, I want to kiss his lips as they sing the beautiful words along with the song. "You look beautiful, by the way."

I beam at him, although I think he would say that if I wore a black bin bag. Any guy that can see me at my worst with sick in my hair and still be interested is a keeper in my book. My stomach sinks as I realise I won't be able to keep him. Once this trip is over, I'll never see him again.

His lips brush my ear. "What happened to you yesterday? Were you avoiding me?"

"No. I was just busy. I went to the spa and then Hilo and had a look around." Even though I was avoiding him after my wax. You're not meant to do anything for twenty-four hours after treatment and after the other night on the balcony, I wouldn't be able to resist his charms.

CHAPTER Ten

LIZZIE

THE SONG ENDS and Ed Sheeran's 'Perfect' plays. Zac holds me close and we sway to the music. With passion bubbling under the surface, I glance at Zac and think how lucky I am that this gorgeous man—scars and all—wants to be with me. He's lucky I feel the same, of course, but I can't ruin this by overthinking. He's not my ex.

"This is nice, Zac. I'm so glad you bunked off work."

"So am I. I've been desperate to do this." His head dips. Our noses touch and our masks clash. He pulls back with a chuckle, abandoning the kiss before our lips met. "That's not how I saw that play out in my head."

"Let's take them off."

"I can't here. I don't want anyone to recognise me. Do you want to go for a walk?"

I nod, then swallow as a lump rises in my throat. I feel like a teenager again, sneaking off for my first kiss.

We step onto the quiet deck, leaving the crowd inside the ballroom. The breeze whips my hair around my face as we walk along the promenade. Zac stops and brushes it to the side with his fingers, then pulls his mask from his head so I can see his striking face and the familiar scars I've come to love.

Love? I draw in a breath. Every cell in my body is ready to burst, tickling my skin. How did this happen? I knew I liked him, but love.

With tentative fingers, he unties the ribbon at the back of my head and the mask I've been wearing slips. "There, that's better."

I feel naked without it, as if he's also peeled away the facade I've been portraying since I arrived on this ship. My legs tremble and my knees weaken.

The masks fall from his fingers, dropping to the deck, and both hands cup my face as he steps closer, warming my body next to his. Desire burns in his eyes, causing my synapses to fire in all directions.

His thumb strokes my cheek, and I whisper his name, "Zachary." I want him, more than I've ever wanted anyone or anything in my entire life. He tilts my head and brings his lips to mine, gently caressing me with his mouth. His tongue slips through, swirling around like the night sky swirls around us, and he takes possession of my mouth, deepening the kiss like he's wanted to do that all night. I close my eyes as my body goes limp against his. The only thing keeping me standing is the railing behind me and his hard chest pressed against me.

A burning heat pulses through me, and I feel brighter than any star in the heavens when I'm with him like this. It's just the two of us, under a blanket of twinkling lights. I could be anywhere in the world with him, and I'd still feel at home. Everything about him just feels so right, like he was made for me or I was made for him. If all we have is tonight, I want to make it last forever.

I come up for air, panting and moaning his name, but

it's barely a whisper. He hears me though, saying my name back like a mantra. "Elizabeth, Elizabeth. My Lizzie." He peppers my face with light kisses as I cling onto him, fisting his shirt to keep steady.

Everything is hazy around me, but I focus on his eyes, taking me deep into the forest. It's burning like wild fire tearing through the trees, and I'm gasping for breath as his mouth smothers mine once more.

His hands are on my body, roaming every inch. He ruffles the long fabric of my red dress, trying to reach the bottom.

"As sexy as you look in this dress, I'm about to rip this fabric in half. I need to have my hands on you. Now." His lips trail my shoulder as he fights with the layers of fabric on my gown.

"Not here," I whisper, but he continues to ruffle the skirt, hiking it up to my waist.

"Zac, not here. We could get caught." With my legs still unsure, I put one foot in front of the other, hoping they don't give way. I take hold of his hand, leading him back into the ship and to my room. He's quiet, his eyes seeping into me, burning through to my core, igniting something deep within; a need, want, longing. I pull the keycard from my small purse and step into my cabin, letting the door automatically close shut.

Before I slip my shoes off, his hands are on me again. His teeth nip my ear, then he sucks my neck. "Lizzie," he growls.

He pushes me down on the bed, making me giggle when I bounce. I lean up on my elbows, watching him unbutton his shirt and catch his lips curl upwards in the corner of his mouth as I pant short hot breaths.

His shirt drops to the floor, and he takes off his belt. With the leather strap in his hand, he creates a loop and snaps it together, making a loud crack.

My heart skips as excitement courses through me. "What are you going to do with that?"

"You'll find out in a minute. Bend over," he growls.

A lump lodges in my throat, and I struggle to speak. "N…no." My eyebrows pull together, and I glare at him. Still panting, I kneel up on the bed with my hands on my hips, but my body fails me as tingles of excitement course through my bloodstream with every snap of his belt.

He throws the leather strap on the dresser and holds up his hands. "I'm just kidding. I'll never hurt you." A grin forms on his face. "Unless you're into that?" He wiggles his eyebrows.

I let out a breath and relax my shoulders. A giggle escapes, and I can't decide if I'm relieved or disappointed.

His smile disappears, and that dark serious look is back. "Take your clothes off, kitten."

I gulp. "Can you help with the dress?" I roll onto my side, moving my hair to the front of my shoulder, giving him access to the zip at the back. He kneels next to me, kisses my neck, and slowly unzips the dress. My limbs tremble as the zip reaches my bottom, revealing my red satin knickers.

He sucks in a breath as he peels away the fabric of my dress, gliding the straps down my arms while planting soft kisses at the back of my neck and shoulder. His lips sail along my spine, sending tingles to my core. I wiggle my hips, and he pulls the dress down, letting it pool around my knees on the bed. His mouth sucks the soft skin of my lower back, and he pulls down the silk, kissing my behind.

"All right, Lizzie, let's get busy."

He playfully slaps my arse, ushering me further up the bed. I smile and lie on my back, watching him stand at the foot and pull his trousers down. His black boxers hug his arse and my eyes fix on the outline of his bulging dick. My breathing quickens, and I'm practically drooling.

Squeezing my thighs together, I feel the dampness soaking into my satin knickers as heat soars from my centre. The cocky smirk on his face has my walls clenching, and my gaze darts back to his boxers as his hand goes under the fabric.

"Take your panties off." His eyes flicker as he fists his erection under his shorts. I do as he asks and lift my bottom to whip them off, but keep my legs together, showing my bare V that I had waxed yesterday.

He stares, crawling on the bed, not taking his eyes off my sex. "Open your legs."

With trembling knees, I pull my legs apart. His fingers stroke from my belly button, down my pillowy stomach and my naked flesh to my slit. My back arches, feeling his finger there, and my chest heaves, lifting my breasts high in my red satin bra.

His lips are close to me, gently working their way up from my thigh while his finger softly runs around my seam. His fierce eyes flash to me. "When did this happen?"

"What?" I pant.

"You waxed your pussy."

"I went to the spa salon yesterday."

"For me?"

"Yes." My voice is shaky. I hope he likes it.

His lips reach my waxed skin. I gasp at his breath on my bare flesh. He replaces his finger with his tongue, slipping it through my folds and down to my entrance. "You didn't have to do this for me. I don't mind a fluffy pussy."

My face heats with embarrassment, but I'm not as embarrassed as I would've been had I not waxed. "I didn't want you stroking my Persian Kitty again."

A puff of laughter leaves his lips and lands on my sensitive area. "But you don't mind me stroking your Brazilian kitty?" His thumb rubs between my folds over the small bud. "You can leave me a landing strip next time."

"Maybe I'll have it shaped into a little heart for you." Why didn't I think of that before? It is Valentine's after all.

"Perhaps I'll do it for you. I have some clippers in my cabin." He flashes me a cheeky grin.

"Stop talking about my pussy. You're embarrassing me."

He plants a delicate kiss against my silky bare skin before his fingers part my lips and he sucks hard on my bundle of nerves. I shudder, fisting the sheets and arch my back as a finger slips inside.

I close my eyes and realise I won't see him the next time I'm due for a wax. I'll be in England, and he'll still be on this ship. My heart aches at the thought of having to say goodbye, but I've always known this is just a holiday fling. I should enjoy it while it lasts and right now I'm enjoying every second. His fingers flicker inside me, and my walls clamp down around him.

"Zac, oh, Zac, don't stop."

"Don't come yet. I want to feel you come around my cock."

I can't not come when he has me like this. My hips buck and I close my eyes. "I can't stop it, Zac." He pulls away, then replaces his fingers with his full length, slamming into me. The way he fills me sends a rush of warmth through my body, coupled with the weight of him on top as he holds himself still and I ride him from the bottom, lifting my hips and rubbing myself against him.

"Open your eyes, kitten. Look at me when I make you come."

My lids open, and he's biting his lip. He's never looked more delicious than hovering above me like this. The pressure builds and I come hard and fast, screaming out. White spots blur my vision, but I see a smirk etched on his gorgeous face as he comes back into focus. My orgasm slows and I slow my hips while catching my breath.

He takes over the rhythm, moving in and out at a fast pace, grinding against me. "You're fucking beautiful, Lizzie."

ZAC

STARING into her eyes while I fuck her makes my body fill with warmth. This is more than fucking. Her pussy clamps down on my dick, and I know she's spent. She slows her hips, and I take over the rhythm.

"Zac," she whimpers as I move my hand to her cheek, my fingers tangle in her golden locks sweet as honey. My other hand holds the headboard as I thrust my hips against her tight pussy.

Fuck. I'm not wearing a rubber. Shit. I can't stop now. Fucking idiot. I was so in the moment it never crossed my mind.

"Are you on the pill, kitten?"

She nods. Thank fuck.

"Do you want me to stop?"

Her legs wrap around me. "No Zac, please don't stop."

"I'm clean, I promise you, but I can pull out if you want me to."

"No, I trust you. I want you inside me, please."

Fuuuck. Hearing her plead like that, I can't stop, and I shoot my load. A grunt leaves my lips, and I thrust again and again, spilling every last drop into her.

Her hands stroke my face and she whimpers my name. "Zachary."

"I know, Lizzie. I know." Can she feel it too? A connection like no other. I haven't had a huge number of different women in my bed, but the ones I've had never felt this good.

I collapse to the side and roll onto my back, catching my breath. She rolls into me and cuddles up to my body. The satin fabric of her bra feels soft against my chest.

"Take this off." I reach behind her and unclip it with one hand; surprising myself. It usually takes me a few attempts. I pull it from her and toss it on the floor. Turning onto my side, I crush her lips, holding her close against my chest. Her fingers graze my jaw as she deepens our kiss.

This woman has me in hot water now. I don't want to think about next week when she's not around anymore. Why the fuck did I sign a contract for nine long-ass months? It feels like a jail sentence now, knowing I could be in England with her.

She pulls her head back slightly, gazing into my eyes. Her thumb swipes over the scar on my top lip. "How did this happen?"

"I was in a motorbike accident."

She sucks in air through her teeth like she can feel the pain from that day. "This as well?" Her fingers touch the scar near my eye.

I nod. "And this." I show her the scars under my tattooed sleeve. "That's why I got the sleeve to hide the scars, hoping I could salvage my modelling career, but nobody would book me with the marks on my face."

She kisses the scar above my lip, then my temple where the other one is. "I'm sorry that happened to you."

"I'm not sorry. If it hadn't happened, I wouldn't be here with you." I smile, hoping I can lighten the mood again. "I'd be famous now, living it up in my Hollywood mansion."

"I didn't know you were a model. Although, I'm not surprised. No wonder you're so bloody cocky." She smiles, and I peck her nose.

"I dropped out of college thinking I could earn more money doing that and buy myself a restaurant. But things never work out how you plan, do they?"

"No, they don't."

"I mean, I never planned on meeting a beautiful lioness who claims she's a kitten, and I certainly never planned this."

"Liar."

"Okay, maybe I planned a little, but it took a week for you to let me in."

"You had me at *nice tits*."

I let out a puff of laughter. "You put up a good fight."

"I was scared of getting hurt again. I still am."

With a sigh, I pull her closer to me and kiss her forehead. "I'll never hurt you, kitten." I know our time together will expire soon, but I'm not gonna let that be the end of us. We'll figure something out. Clasping her hand in mine, I hold it against the swallow on my chest. "Swallows mate for life, don't they?"

CHAPTER
Eleven

LIZZIE

THE SUNLIGHT POURS in through the balcony doors as I open my eyes and close them again. Rolling over, my chest bangs into a solid warm mass, reminding me of last night. I blink away the sleep and gaze at his perfect naked body.

Zac lies on his stomach with his hands tucked underneath the pillow. The duvet covers his arse, and I glide my hand down his spine and under the blanket, brushing it from him so I can get a better view. I shuffle my body closer to his with my arm draped over him and my hand squeezing his cheek.

He stirs and blinks open his eyes. "Is it morning already?"

"Hmm. I wish it was still last night."

He rolls onto his side and pulls me flush with his body so my breasts crush against his chest. "Last night was fucking awesome." His warm lips press against mine in a long hard kiss. He releases my mouth and gazes at me.

"You're beautiful, you know. Even first thing in a morning, you're so fucking beautiful." His hand slips between my thighs, and I'm already wet.

"I need a shower."

"You're only gonna get messy again. Just have one

after." He rolls me onto my back and trails kisses down my neck.

"Zac."

He groans as his lips navigate down the valley of my breasts while squeezing with his hand and pinching my nipple.

"Zac, stop."

He halts, tearing his lips away and lifts himself, hovering above me. "You weren't saying that last night."

"We weren't docked in a port last night." I nod towards the sliding doors of the balcony. We never closed the curtains last night as we were out at sea, but this morning, I can see people walking around the dock in the distance.

Zac drops his head and chuckles, kissing my nose. "You had me worried then. Don't move." He jumps out of bed stark naked, holding a cushion in front of his morning wood as he walks over to the sliding glass doors, and pulls the curtains closed.

I check the time on my phone. "Zac it's almost 10am."

"So."

"So I have a trip booked." I throw the blanket off my body and dart into the bathroom, grabbing the robe.

Zac stands in the doorway, still naked and hard, leaning against the doorjamb with his arm up. "What time's your trip?"

"10.30am." I place some toothpaste on my toothbrush and scrub my teeth while my eyes rake his tanned body.

"What trip?"

"The waterfalls tour." I say with a mouthful of foamy toothpaste.

"You won't make it. Come back to bed." He wraps his arms around me from behind while I wash my face.

"I will if I hurry. When the coach leaves in thirty minutes, I need to be on it."

"Spend the day with me instead." His hot mouth plants kisses on my neck, and I feel him grinding his thick erection into my arse. As much as I would love to spend the day with him, I'm done allowing a man to dictate my life and stop me from living my dreams.

"Don't you have to work? You're not pulling another sickie, are you?"

"I start work at five today. We can spend the full day together."

"No, I paid for this trip, and I've been excited about seeing the island since I booked it. I'll never get the chance to see it again."

He lets go of me. "And you'll never get the chance to spend the day with me, either. You'll be back in England in less than a week." He huffs, storming out of the bathroom, slamming the door behind him.

My chest aches. What's the point of this? He's right, of course, but for that same reason, what's the point in spending the day with him to get more attached and get lost deeper in that forest? I pin my hair up and jump in the shower for a quick wash. It's better this way. My heart pangs, but we had fun. Better to end it now than later.

I step out of the shower, pulling on the robe and check the time. I have fifteen minutes. Zac's gone. I don't have time to worry about him or chase after him. I dress in my bikini and throw a floral summer dress over the top.

Grabbing my bag, I chuck some makeup in there and run a comb through my curls.

With a heavy heart, I slip on my flat sandals and race to catch the coach, sprinting down the flights of stairs towards the exit. A hoard of women in lycra, block the stairway as they exit the yoga studio. Who comes on holiday to do yoga?

"Excuse me." Squeezing through the crowd, I get a few snarky looks, but I don't care, and barge through the herd. I don't need to check my phone to know it's gone half past the hour, and I just hope the coach has waited for me. An elevator door dings opens, and I think I'll be quicker getting the lift rather than running down another two flights of stairs.

An older lady steps in with me and presses a button. "Going up?"

"I'm going down, please."

The lift travels in the wrong direction. My hair sticks to my neck, and I grip the handles of my beach bag as a huff blows through my gritted teeth. Is the universe telling me something? I could have still been in bed right now, pressed next to Zac's warm body. I could have spent the entire day like that. This isn't my finest hour, all so I could see a pissin' waterfall. I can view them on the internet. And now I don't have either. I sigh heavily and slump against the mirror in the lift.

"Everything all right, dear?"

I tap my foot while chewing on the inside of my mouth. No lady, nothing is all right. I've just pissed off the first guy I've had in my bed that actually knows how to treat a woman and now, thanks to you, I will probably have missed my trip to the waterfalls.

"Yes, thank you," I say with a clenched jaw and put on a fake smile.

The lift comes to a halt, and she steps off. I press the button before anyone else jumps in and the lift descends, along with my stomach. I wipe my top lip and brow where beads of moisture gather and finally; the lift comes to a stop.

As I step off, I rush down the stairway. The morning rush of holidaymakers taking excursions are nowhere to be seen, and neither is a coach. An attendee informs me the coach left ten minutes ago. Stomping across the dock with tears building, I silently scream and slam my hand against the metal railing, then wince, shaking away the pain.

As I stand on the dockside clutching my beach bag, I turn to see Zac across the dock, leaning against the opposite railings. I can't quite see his facial expression to see if he's still upset with me, but when he strides over, breaking into a jog half way, my breath hitches as a rainbow bursts in my chest. He bundles me up in his arms and I sag against him, resting my cheek in the crevice of his neck and shoulder. The warmth from his skin soothes me, along with his usual scent mixed with mine from last night.

I know he'll just think I want to spend the day with him because I've nothing better to do, but the truth is, I would have chosen him a hundred times over if I thought this would go anywhere, but I'm no fool. I know this is just a bit of fun. He probably has a different girl on every cruise, and I'm the chosen one for the fortnight. I'm scared to let myself feel anything for him, even though I feel everything for him, and it's probably too late for me.

I blink, letting the tears drip from my lashes. My fist grips his t-shirt, and he rubs my back as I sniffle and shudder, letting out a sob.

Cupping my face, he pulls away to look at me. "You wanted to see those waterfalls, huh?" His thumbs swipe under my eyes, wiping the tears.

I let out a sigh. "I'm not upset about the bus, the trip, or whatever. I'm just happy that you're here."

A puff of air escapes his mouth. "Happy? You could have fooled me." He brings me back to his shoulder again and kisses my head. "I'm sorry I stormed out. I wasn't angry. My ego was hurt, that's all."

"I'm sorry."

"I have an idea." Holding my hand, he leads me away from the ship. The smell of fish and diesel fill the air as we make our way through the dock. After a fifteen-minute walk, we arrive at a car garage with a hire shop. Zac enters like he knows them. He's probably been here a hundred times already. A big guy comes to the counter. "What can I do for you today?"

"We'd like a jeep, please." Zac pulls out his wallet and hands over his driving licence and credit card. He fills out some forms, then the shop guy walks into the back and returns, jangling keys.

"This one has a full tank of fuel." He leads us to the courtyard with an array of vehicles and shows us to an old jeep. Zac takes the keys and thanks the guy.

I slide into the passenger side and close the door. My

stomach bubbles like water in a Jacuzzi at the excitement of going for a drive with him. Right now, though, after seeing him at the dockside waiting for me, he could have taken me back to the room or anywhere, and I wouldn't care as long as I was with him.

He gets into the driver's seat. I pull my seatbelt on and buckle up. He checks the buckle tugging on the belt, making sure I'm strapped in. His breath lands on my cheek, and I bite my lip to stop me from ravishing him in the car lot. He sits back and buckles himself in before revving the engine. Nodding at the guy, he drives off the yard and down the road.

"Where are we going?"

"You'll see." He flashes a smile, shifts gear, then places his hand on mine, which rests in my lap. The gesture is so simple, but it makes my legs tingle and turn to jelly like they did last night. The memory of him still lingers between my thighs; that delicious feeling of being stretched and full and warm, like when you're satisfied after a good meal. I interlace my fingers with his and grip his hand, etching this moment into my mind to treasure for years to come.

We drive up a steep incline. The luscious green hills roll all around us, and the view behind is a ribbon of sparkling azur ocean. Zac shifts into a lower gear and the jeep slows, struggling to get up the hill. I look out of the window at the drop next to me and gasp. No railings or health and safety like there is in Britain, just a drop at the side of the road. One false move from Zac, and it's all over for both of us. A lump catches in my throat and lodges there. My chest heaves with short, quick breaths.

"You all right?" Zac rubs a thumb over my thigh.

"Just keep your eyes on the road."

He chuckles. "Don't worry. I've driven up here plenty of times."

My stomach rolls. "I don't want to know how many women you've brought up here."

"You're the first girl I've done this with."

My head flinches back and I wrinkle my brow. "You don't have to lie. it's fine. I'd just rather not know." I shake the thought.

"Hey, I'm telling the truth. Usually, there's a group of us from the ship when we have a day off." He squeezes my thigh and the phantom throb between my legs from last night returns.

Trees line the valley, and a stream cuts into the hill, making its way down to the ocean. My shoulders relax as we reach the top, and steer away from the drop onto a flatter road.

After driving down a dirt path for another ten minutes, he parks in the middle of the trees. "We hike the rest of the way." He unbuckles the seat belt and steps out.

Gripping my bag, I follow his lead. "How far?" I look down at my flat sandals. They're not really suitable for hiking.

Zac takes my hand. "You're fine. It's not far." We walk through the trees, pushing through the foliage. Twigs snap underfoot, and the branches rustle in the gentle breeze. The sun peers through the trees, and steam rises from the dew, coating my skin in a cold, sticky sweat. I breathe in the fresh scent of wet earth mixed with the cool mountain air.

Zac's hand grips mine tight like he's never going to let me go. After last night, I want that. I want to be his and spend days together with him like this. Though I should never have slept with him last night, knowing once I did I would be a gonner. One-nighters aren't for me. I get too emotionally involved. *Stop overthinking and just enjoy what little time you have left.*

His strides are longer than mine. My chubby legs struggle to keep up.

"What's the rush?" I say, short of breath. He smiles and pauses, noticing how unfit I am. He doesn't speak and just kisses me hard, forcing me against a tree.

CHAPTER *Twelve*

ZAC

I COULD TAKE her right here. One hand rests against the tree trunk, my other trails up her thigh to her ass while I smother her sweet moans with my mouth. I've wanted her ever since I woke up hard as a rock this morning.

My dick throbs in my jeans, and I straighten to adjust myself, wishing I'd put shorts on instead of grabbing the nearest thing before running to catch the bus. She wasn't escaping me so easily. I never even showered this morning. Her sex still clings to my body, and I can still taste her in my mouth.

A rustle in the bushes jolts my head back. I train my ears to where the sound is coming from. Branches crack, then voices come into earshot as a group of tourists approach.

Lizzie takes my hand, and we carry on the descent. "Is that what you got me up here for? We could have returned to the room."

"That's not why I brought you up here. Although it would make the day a lot more fun." I tease.

She bumps my shoulder but doesn't say no. The hikers head on in front at a faster pace. I slow my steps down so she can keep at my side without breaking into a sprint. She looks at me through her lashes with eyes so blue they remind me of the lagoon I'm taking her to.

My chest aches that in less than a week I won't have those baby blues to look at or see that smile of hers light up the restaurant when she sees me. Out of all the women I've flirted with on a ship, there's something about her that draws me in. We live such different lives and yet we're one of the same.

I watch her face beam as we approach a clearing and the waterfall comes into view. She never fails to surprise me, like I'm unwrapping a parcel and each layer reveals something new until I reach the heart of her. I find it hard to believe that a rich woman like her has lived such a sheltered life, but I'm grateful I can give her these firsts.

A smile is etched on her face as she looks at me with bright eyes and then back to the view, gasping at the lagoon, surrounded by luscious green hills and volcanic rocks.

"Zac, it's beautiful."

I behold the water cascading off the cliff into the pool below and then gaze back at her gleaming face. While the scene is beautiful, it's nothing compared to her. The way her eyes glisten in the sun and her lips spread across her face, pushing her flushed cheeks up, makes my heart sing, then my cock joins the party and wants to dance.

"Can we go down?"

"Yeah, there are some wooden steps over here." I point to the logs built into the side of the hill, creating a stairway down to the water. A couple of locals jump off the cliff and plunge down in front of the waterfall. Hikers settle on the water's edge and take out snacks from their backpacks.

Another family picnic on the grass nearby and a group of girls are sunbathing next to the lagoon.

Lizzie pulls out her phone and starts snapping photos, turning around to capture me as I walk behind her.

"Watch your step. It's slippery." I hold her hand, guiding her downwards.

"I love this, Zac."

I imagine her saying that she loves me. I know I've only known her a week, but I'd like to hear her speak those words someday.

"Thank you." She kisses my cheek.

Hunger for her burns in the pit of my stomach. After a rocky start this morning, I think we're back on track.

We reach the bottom of the lagoon and walk along the grassy bank to a quiet area near the waterfall. The gushing water is a constant soothing to my soul. I always loved it up here, though in previous years there weren't so many tourists.

She pulls a rolled towel from her bag and looks at me. "I only have the one."

I shrug. "We'll have to share then." A smirk forms on my face, and she smiles that beautiful bright smile of hers. She slips her sandals off and takes off her clothes, highlighting her sexy, full figure in a floral bikini.

Kneeling on the towel, she bends over. Her perfectly round ass is in my face. I want to whip her bottoms off and sink my teeth into that ripe peach. My mouth waters. Truth be told, I've thought of nothing else all week.

She holds out a bottle of sunblock. "Will you put my sun cream on, please?"

I take it from her, happy to oblige, but before I do, I

whip my top off and lather my shoulders and chest before I start on her.

She leans back on her heels, and I kneel behind her. Moving her blonde hair to the side, it flows down the front of her body. My fingers sail from her ear, down her neck before I replace them with my lips, navigating gentle kisses along her shoulder. Her soft skin against my lips and the honey scent of her hair has my body firing on all cylinders.

I slide my palms down the bare skin of her arm and she hums, tilting her head to allow me access to more of her neck. My tongue licks below her ear and I suck delicately, brushing my lips against her, and whisper, "I want you, Lizzie."

Her hand moves to my face, rubbing her palm against my unshaven jaw. She wraps her fingers around my neck and moves her head to meet my lips.

Breaking the kiss with panting breaths, my eyes wander to her tits, brimming over the top of her bikini. I want to whip it off and fill my fingers with that soft, bouncy flesh. She's fucking perfect. Every part of her is perfect, but most of all, I love the way she looks at me. She sees past all my flaws and sees my soul that's been searching for her and I never even knew.

"I want you too, Zac. And I don't just mean here and now." Her eyes gaze upon my face and her finger caresses the scar on my temple before moving to the one above my lip. "I want you, all of you, all the time."

I close my eyes and rest my forehead against hers. I'm not any good at the long distance thing, but I'm willing to try for her until my contract's up. Not sure what to say, I smother her mouth with a searing kiss.

After pouring some lotion on my hands, I work it into her back, massaging her muscles over the swallow on her shoulder. I kneel up and reach over her to massage the lotion into her chest. She sucks in a breath as my fingers delve beneath the fabric of her bikini and find her nipple. With both hands I tweak the nubs until they're both erect and crying out for my mouth.

My cock stiffens, like it's on the same wavelength, and I need to adjust my jeans again. Why didn't I wear shorts? I'm so hot, my jeans are sticking to me, but this is nice, being out here with her. My dick will just have to wait.

She drops her head back against my shoulder, closing her eyes, and lets out another light moan. My cock perks up again, like he can hear her.

Two swallows appear on a rock next to us. "Lizzie, look."

"Oh, are they mating?"

One keeps swooping down and landing on the other. "I think they are."

She giggles. "I've never seen that before, only on the discovery channel."

"It's a sign." I kiss her neck.

She turns her head to meet my lips.

"Lie down for me, kitten."

She lies back on the towel, and I position myself between her legs. I kiss her soft stomach, then rub the sunblock into her skin, tucking my fingers under the elastic of her panties ever so slightly. My eyes gaze into hers, bluer than the lagoon right in front of us, but deeper than the deepest ocean. I work my way down her leg, rubbing the lotion into her calve and glide my hand back up between her thighs, massaging over her inked garter as I go. My thumb grazes over her bikini bottoms at the apex of her thighs.

She pants, arching her back. "Zac," she whispers.

I graze my fingers over her again, and she lets out a ragged breath. Her body trembles with every stroke of my hand. I've never wanted anyone more than I want her in this moment, quivering under me, or on top of my dick.

"In the water. Now."

She leans up on her elbows. "What for?"

My hands grip her thighs, digging my fingers into her plump flesh as I am about to lose all self-control. "I'm about ten seconds from ripping these bottoms off and sinking myself so deep into you, you won't be able to walk for a week. So either we do it here and risk a fine, or we go in the water and be more discreet."

Her eyes widen. She gulps, but her panting breaths tell me she's feeling everything I'm feeling.

"Now, princess," I growl.

She scrambles to obey and crawls to the edge of the lagoon. "Is it deep?"

"It is in the middle." I stand and climb onto a rock and jump in. The cool water shocks my skin, but it's a welcome change from the searing heat on this volcanic island. My jeans are heavy on my legs, like a weight pulling me down, and I wish I hadn't gone commando this morning. "Come to the edge of the rock. I'll help you in."

She crawls onto the black volcanic rock, dangling her legs over the edge. I hold my arms out for her, and she lets herself fall onto me. We both bob under the surface and swim back up together with her arms wrapped around my neck. I gaze at her face as the sun shines down on us. Her blonde hair is slicked back from the water and the dusting of freckles across her nose becomes more prominent every day.

I peck her lips. She wraps her legs around my waist, and I tread water for the both of us. Her trembles match my own rugged breathing as our kiss deepens, and I need to remove the barrier between us; her bikini and my jeans.

"Let's go behind the waterfall."

She looks over at the cascade from the cliff top. A guy yells as he jumps in front and crashes into the gushing fall, followed by cheers and claps.

"In the cavern," I tell her. "They won't see us."

She nods, and we both swim towards the curtain of water. Tiny droplets dust us in a cool mist, then a thundering shower pummels against us as we push through into a carved out cavern behind the veil, taking my breath away.

My eyes adjust to the dull cave, but light shines through the falling water, creating a spectrum of dancing shapes all around us. I lift myself onto a submerged rock and sit back, pulling her on top of me. The clear constant flow of water laps around my waist, and goosebumps coat my skin, but I'm not sure if it's the cooler temperature in the cavern or her.

She unzips my jeans. The soaked denim sticks to my ass, making it hard to peel them off, but nothing could stop me from having her. With every ounce of strength I have, I yank them down in one swoop.

Her tits press into my face as she straddles me, and I unclip her bikini top. It falls from her arms between us, and I engulf her pebbled nipple into my mouth. She grinds her hips against me, our bodies flush, and even though the cascade from above is deafening, I can still hear her heart beating next to mine.

My hands dive under the fabric and squeeze her ass. "Take your panties off for me, kitten."

She stands on the rock, the water laps around her knees as she wiggles her hips, pulling down the lycra bottoms. I hook my arm through the leg so they don't drift away, and with her bare pussy in front of my face, I grab her ass, forcing her to my mouth so I can taste her again. My tongue runs between her folds, and she moans, fisting my hair. Her legs tremble as my tongue flicks her little nub and I groan against her, sending a vibration around her pussy that has her at my mercy, panting my name.

CHAPTER Thirteen

LIZZIE

ANOTHER MOAN ESCAPES ME, louder this time, echoing around the small cavity. I'm suddenly aware of my surroundings and sit down before anyone sees me naked. I take his tongue in my mouth instead. As much as I wanted him to carry on with his tender assault, it was too risky.

My heart pounds, matching the hammering of the waterfall as it hits the rocks, and the spray cools my body from the searing heat between us. The light shining through the water gives the cave a soft rippling glow, highlighting the need in Zac's face.

I rub my slick opening against his throbbing erection and after several strokes, he pushes through my walls until we're clasped together like two pieces of a jigsaw. His hands grip my arse cheeks, rocking me at a pace that matches his shallow breaths. The bristles from his unshaven jaw rub against my skin as he greedily tastes me deeper.

He breaks our kiss and his lips move to my chest. His jaw rubs against the soft flesh of my breasts, but with every scratch from his stubble, a tender kiss follows with a lick of his tongue and a suck from his mouth as his lips navigate the valley of my cleavage.

The pressure builds in the pit of my stomach and the tingling pulses through my core with each rock of my hips. I'm close. "Zac."

He growls into my breast and squeezes my arse.

"Zac." I pant, lifting his head so I can gaze into his eyes that are greener than the Hawaiian hills. "I want you to look at me when I make you come," I say his own words back to him from the other night when he had me at his mercy under the blanket of stars. Now I'm in control. I rock my hips faster.

He quirks a grin but doesn't break eye contact. "Whatever you say, princess."

Our eyes connect. Our breathing is in rhythm, sucking in each other's air, and my head swims. I'm in paradise and not because of this beautiful setting. It's him. He takes me to the heavens, leaving the idyllic setting of the Hawaiian valley to soar over the Elysian fields.

"I need you to come now, kitten." His eyes plead with me as the struggle to hold back shows in his clenched jaw. "Come. Now," he growls.

My nails dig into his back. I widen my eyes as a wave of satisfaction bursts through every cell. I cry out into his mouth. My limbs shake and with it my body slows the rocking rhythm. Zac takes over, thrusting from the bottom and groans. His eyelashes flicker, but he holds my gaze.

In my entire adult life, I don't think there's ever been anything sexier than watching this man fall apart with me. What's he doing to me? I know he's going to break my heart and here I am, continuing down a path I know is not good, but it feels so right. This will end one way or another. He works on a cruise ship and I have to return home. I shake the thought. I don't want to think about that now.

My arms wrap around his neck, and I press my face against his cheek. "I never want to let you go."

Voices echo in the cavern, and a woman pokes through the wall of water. Zac pulls me tight against his chest, shielding my breasts. The woman's eyes rest on us, and my knickers hooked on Zac's arm. An expression of horror washes over her face, and she ushers her two children back and retreats behind the waterfall as quickly as she came.

A giggle bursts from my lips, and Zac chuckles into my mouth, kissing me in between puffs of laughter. "I should put my bikini top back on." I look between us, lift myself from him and search the small pool we're sitting in.

Zac hands me my bottoms.

"Have you hid my top?" I giggle as I pop my bikini bottoms back on.

He searches the area. "No, I haven't." He struggles to pull up his drenched jeans.

"Come on, just hand me my bra and stop fooling around."

"Lizzie, honestly, I don't have it." Zac chuckles, but the puzzled expression on his face as he searches the pool bed tells me he's being honest.

My heart beats rapidly, like a fish caught in a net. I cover my breasts, folding my arms across them. My body has cooled, but my cheeks are burning up. I can almost feel the steam escaping from my damp hair. "What shall I do?"

Zac stands and kisses my forehead. "Don't worry. I'll get you my t-shirt. Wait here." He climbs the rock where we came in and disappears through the veil of water that pours down into the lagoon. After a few minutes, he returns with his white t-shirt, which is now partially wet. I take it from him and pull it over my head.

The fabric stretches around my breasts, making it even more opaque; combined with the wet patches, I may as well not bother wearing it at all. "I look like I'm entering a wet t-shirt competition."

"Sweetheart, you would win it hands down."

I splash water on his face. "If there was a competition for an annoying waiter, you'd get first prize."

"What have I done now?"

"I'm sure you've hidden my bikini top so you can ogle my breasts for the rest of the day."

He chuckles. "I haven't, I promise."

"Liar, just like you didn't spill your drink on me the other night so you could get me naked in your room. Hmmm?"

"Again, that was an accident. I swear."

"And what about when you dropped the icing sugar all down your trousers? You wanted me to see how big your dick was. Admit it." I fold my arms, tapping my fingers against my skin.

"I'm innocent. What can I say? You make me nervous." He pecks my nose.

"That was my favourite bikini as well."

"You look good in my t-shirt though."

We swim back to the side of the lagoon. I know I've only known him a week, but I feel like I've known him my whole life, like we were meant to meet on this trip.

"I've had an amazing day today."

"It's been so much better than some organised tour, right?"

"Yes, I'm so glad I saw you on the dock."

A child's voice cries out from across the lagoon. "Mummy, look what I found." He holds up my bikini top, waving it in the air like a flag.

My breath hitches and my skin pricks as a flush of heat creeps up my neck.

Zac bursts out laughing. "At least you can't blame me for hiding it now." He walks to the edge of the water, about to jump in.

"What are you doing?"

"Going to get your top from that kid."

"Don't you dare." I make a grab for his arm, but he swims over and talks to the woman.

I hastily dive into the bushes, parting the leaves, and peek out.

The woman's gaze snaps to mine and I hide under a palm.

Zac returns with a grin still painted on his face. "Here you go. It took a bit of convincing. The boy wanted it as a catapult!"

BACK AT THE SHIP, Zac heads to work, and I change for dinner.

Walking towards the lift, the redhead from the orientation comes towards me. "Ah, Miss Jones. I was sorry you decided not to join us on the excursion today. Why didn't you cancel sooner and collect your refund?"

"I didn't cancel. I missed the bus."

"We were waiting for you, and Zac said you'd made other arrangements. We always wait at least fifteen minutes for any late arrivals."

"Zac said what?"

"You told him you weren't going on the trip, right?"

A lump lodges in my throat, and a layer of sweat coats my skin as my entire body tenses. "Zac told you I was cancelling the excursion?"

"He said you'd made other plans with him, and we didn't need to wait for you, so the coach set off. Is that not the case? It's just because you didn't cancel within the allocated time, I can't offer you a refund."

My nostrils flare and my teeth grind together, but as angry as I am, I don't want Zac to get in trouble. "That's fine. I just changed my plans at the last minute. I'm sorry," I say through clenched teeth. My fists ball around my clutch purse. How could he do that? Who the hell does he think he is? No man controls my life.

"No harm done. I hope you enjoyed your day. And don't worry, I won't say anything about you and Zac." The redhead walks off down the corridor.

After these new revelations, the day has left a bitter residue in my mouth. I stomp down the atrium, breathing heavily through my nostrils while chewing on the inside of my mouth.

All dolled up in my cute lemon dress just for him, I wait in line at the Italian restaurant. My nostrils flare when I spot him. He smiles at me, waving his hand, and I want to scream.

Arrgghh. I will blow my top in the middle of the

restaurant if I stay here. Smacking him in the mouth is high on my agenda right now. I sigh, knowing I would kiss it better afterwards. No. I won't allow another man to push me around and tell me what to do. I'm an independent woman. I stomp off through the atrium and step into the lift. My knuckles are white from gripping my purse so tight.

"What level, dear?" An older lady asks.

"The next floor, please. The buffet restaurant."

CHAPTER Fourteen

ZAC

"WHERE DID LIZZIE GO?" I ask Josh on my way to serve another table.

He checks the room. "She never came in."

"But she was here a moment ago." Wasn't she? Am I just imagining it? I'm sure I saw her; a vision in lemon, like a rare yellow Hawaiian hibiscus. The bright colour set off her golden hair and her skin was glowing from the sun today.

I check the bookings at the front desk. Her name is still unticked, confirming she hasn't arrived. Perhaps she went to the ladies' room. She didn't smile at me, though. Was she trying to tell me something? I hope she's feeling well.

When my shift is finally over, I make my way to her cabin, needing to check she's all right. I knock on the door. "Lizzie." There's no answer. I knock again. "Kitten, are you in there?" My knocks fall on deaf ears, and I slump against the door, waiting for her, wherever she is. My head leans back against the frame, and I close my eyes. Before I know it, my lids grow heavy, and I'm drifting off. It's been a long day.

"What are you doing?" A harsh voice jolts me awake. I

open my eyes to Lizzie hovering above me with a hand on her hip and the other clutching her purse. Her face is beautiful, but her eyebrows pinch together, and her lips press into a thin, hard line.

"What's it look like? I'm waiting for you. Where have you been?"

She waves her purse in front of my face. "What's it to you? You want to cancel my plans again?"

With confusion filling my mind, I jump to my feet. "What the hell are you talking about?"

"You know exactly what I'm talking about. You cancelled my trip this morning." Her fists dig into her hips as she breathes out through flared nostrils like a fierce dragon ready to give me a roasting.

"I nev—"

She cuts me off. I daren't talk over her in case she burns me at the stake. "You were there when the bus was waiting for me, and you told them I wasn't coming. How could you do that?"

"I did—"

She cuts me off again. "You had no right to cancel my trip."

I clench my jaw. If she's so unwilling to listen to my explanation, she doesn't deserve one. "I seem to recall you had a pretty fucking spectacular day. What the fuck are you complaining for?"

Her purse whacks me in the chest. "I would have had an awesome day, with or without you. That trip was a once in a lifetime opportunity."

Ouch. Her words tear into me like an iceberg ripping

open the hull of a ship. "And I wasn't? You'll never get the chance to have me again, sweetheart." My lip twitches as I try to restrain myself from lashing out and my heart sinks to my stomach, causing a sudden spout of nausea.

"I will never want you again. I just got rid of one controlling arsehole. I don't want another."

"Is that what you think of me?" Damn, now I feel used. So I'm good for a screw when she has nothing better to do. When she was late, I hoped she'd changed her mind and wanted to spend the day with me. What a fucking idiot. My body tenses. Each time she yells at me, my heart sinks further as another word cuts deep.

"What do you expect when you cancel my plans without my permission? How dare you?"

"Excuse me for wanting to spend a day with you. What's wrong with that? You even said you were glad you missed the bus." She doesn't know the truth or the real reason I was on the dock, but she doesn't seem to care. I'm not going to correct her now. It's like she's already made her mind up about me and isn't willing to give me the benefit of the doubt.

"Before I knew you made me miss it. My last boyfriend thought he could tell me to jump, and I would say how high. I'm not doing that again."

"Good, because I'm not your boyfriend, princess." I spit the words out, then storm down the corridor before I say something else I'll regret, or worse, do something I regret, like drag her into the cabin and fuck her until she calms down. My fists clench into tight balls as I stomp to my room. Did she use me for a good time? She isn't like that. Is she?

LIZZIE

I DON'T SEE Zac today. In fact, I avoid him like the plague. I'm still annoyed with him, but what made it worse was that he never even apologised. How can he think what he did was actually okay?

The sad thing is that if he had said, 'Forget the trip, I'll take you to see the waterfalls,' I would've gone with him in a heartbeat. But I wasn't about to miss out on an excursion I had paid good money for, to stay in bed with him in the cabin all day.

I dress up again for dinner, for nobody other than myself this time. I don't intend on eating in the Italian restaurant tonight.

As I step out of my cabin, Kenna is there.

"Hi, Elizabeth."

"Hello, Kenna, do you want to go for dinner?"

"I'm having a meal with Domo tonight in his suite."

My heart sinks at the thought of another meal alone. "Sounds lovely."

"What's wrong?"

"Nothing. You enjoy your meal."

"Something's not right with you. Tell me what's wrong?"

"Zac and I had a fight. That's all, nothing really. I mean, I wasn't going to see him after next week anyway, but—"

"Come and eat with us. Domo won't mind."

"Oh no, Kenna. I couldn't intrude on your romantic meal."

"Please, his bodyguard will probably be there. It won't be that romantic." She giggles, then links her arm through mine and pulls me down the corridor.

"You're really strong for a tiny woman, aren't you?"

"And very persuasive."

We step into the lift, and Kenna presses the button for deck seven. "Tell me all about this fight."

I tell her what happened, and she agrees with me, telling me I have every right to be upset and pats me on the back for standing my ground.

Domo's bodyguard stands outside the owner's suite and opens the door as we approach. "He's expecting you, ma'am, but not your friend here."

"I'll smooth it over with him. This is Elizabeth. She's harmless. You gonna let us in, or do you want to frisk her first?" Kenna stands with her hands on her hips, like a force of nature.

Another guy in a suit comes into view and nods at the bodyguard, waving us in.

He tilts his head, cracking his neck. "Go ahead, ma'am."

"Thank you," I say, stepping into the suite. I thought I had a luxury cabin, but this is something else. The other guy must be Domo, as he seems to be the boss around here. He's talking in a foreign language into a mobile handset with a wrinkle on his brow that disappears when he locks eyes with Kenna. His face lights up until he sees me standing behind her, shuffling on my feet.

He kills the call and stares at Kenna, waiting for an introduction.

"Domo, this is my friend and neighbour, Elizabeth. I said she could join us for dinner, rather than spend it alone."

"The more the merrier." His silver eyes soften, changing to a warm grey, sparkling when he smiles. "Let me get you ladies a drink. You like champagne, Elizabeth?"

"Yes, please." He pours two glasses of champagne and pops a strawberry on the side of the glass. "Thank you," I say as he hands it to me.

"Let me show Elizabeth the balcony," Kenna says.

I follow her out onto the large veranda, which is equally as large as the suite, encompassing a table and chairs and several sun loungers. My eyes wander all around and up at the evening sky, sipping my champagne. It really is like drinking the stars. An expensive bottle, no doubt.

This entire suite oozes opulence. How the other half live. I feel like Grace Kelly, rubbing shoulders with the rich and famous, especially in my elegant cream dress. "This is just beautiful, Kenna. I thought our suites were nice, but this is another world."

"Our cabins are just below."

I snap my head back to her and swallow. "My cabin is underneath this one?" I bend over the balcony, trying to get a look at the one below.

She nods her head, making her spirals bounce around her face, which is glowing a warm brown. Did she hear me

ANNIE CHARME

the other night? My cheeks heat and I take a large gulp of champagne to cool myself down and the bubbles fizz up my nose.

I gasp. Frozen, my eyes bulge. That was her the other night. My heart races and I take another drink, but all I can picture is Kenna and Domo out here on the veranda. I shake my head, trying to erase the vision in my mind and gaze up at the night sky instead.

Domo steps outside with the bottle of champagne in his hand. "Would you like a top-up, Elizabeth?"

I glance at my drink, virtually empty, and hold it out with a trembling hand. "Yes please, da—Domo."

He tops me up and his bodyguard joins us, following him like a shadow wherever he goes. I smile, wondering if his bodyguard was here the other night.

I follow Domo and Kenna into the dining room. A large oval table sits in the centre. The room is geared up for meetings and conferences, but tonight the table is adorned with candles and flowers.

Domo pulls my chair out, and I take a seat. He does the same for Kenna, smiling at her the entire time like a cute puppy dog where she's concerned.

A waiter walks in holding a silver platter of appetisers, followed by another waiter. My heart stills when Zac appears. His eyes narrow into thin slits when he sees me, tensing his body as he grips a bottle of wine.

Bypassing me, he walks over to Domo. "Chateau Lafite, sir."

Domo nods at Zac who takes his wine glass and fills it with red wine. Moving to Kenna. "Madam?"

"Yes, please."

Zac fills Kenna's glass.

"Thank you."

He ignores me and walks past me towards the door.

"Excuse me. You forgot Elizabeth," Domo says.

Zac turns to me with daggers in his eyes.

I look between him and Domo. "It's fine, I'll drink water."

Domo stands. "It's not fine. He isn't doing his job properly."

"He'll probably spill it on me anyway," I huff.

Zac snatches my glass from the table. His hand shakes as he pours, and he furrows his brow, trying to keep a steady flow. He slides the glass back to me and stares with a clenched jaw before disappearing out of the room.

"Excuse me." I stand and follow him into the corridor. "What's your problem?"

"What are you doing here with Daddy-fucking-Warbucks?"

"His name is Domo. Did you know that was him from the balcony the other night?"

"Sure I did. Everyone knows Mr Nilsen is staying in the owner's suite. Are you fucking him now?"

"Don't be ridiculous." I huff and place my hands on my hips.

"You got off listening to them on the balcony. You want a turn."

"I don't sleep with just anybody."

"Huh, you dropped your knickers for me."

I slap him across the face. "How dare you?" He wasn't

just anybody to me. I actually liked him, until I realised what a possessive, controlling arsehole he is.

He rubs his cheek. His eyes are dull and lifeless, like someone has just turned off a light switch.

"You don't know me at all."

"I don't want to know you, if this is how you behave."

"How I behave? You embarrassed me in there. I'm having a meal with friends, not a gang-bang. Besides, what about your behaviour? You haven't even apologised for cancelling my tour."

"I won't apologise for wanting to spend time with the woman I…"

I hold my breath, waiting for him to finish his sentence. He doesn't say anything more, and just stares at me, breathing hard.

"The woman you what? Tell me what you were going to say."

"The woman I'm fucking. This week anyway."

Tears prick my eyes and a lump forms in the back of my throat as I choke out words. "You're an arsehole. I wish I'd never laid eyes on you."

"Good thing we won't see each other after next week, then." He turns and walks away, leaving me alone. A tear rolls down my cheek, and I dab it away with my cream shawl, not wanting to ruin my makeup or my night. I'm more mad at myself for getting emotional over a man after a week, or ten days, or whatever it's been. I vowed to never lose myself to a man again, and here I am wearing my heart on my sleeve once more. With a heavy heart, I walk back into the room and sit at the table next to Kenna.

"Everything all right, hon?"

I nod and give her a fake smile.

"Want me to have him fired?" Domo asks.

"Don't tempt me." But as much as I hate him right now, I don't want to jeopardise his position on board. If only he'd apologised, I would have forgiven him, but after tonight I'm not so sure.

CHAPTER
Fifteen

ZAC

THE FLOOR MOVES under my feet, and I feel the gentle sway from side to side. I balance the drinks on the tray and hold it with two hands as I make my way to table nine. A loved up couple sit holding hands and gazing into each other's eyes, reminding me of Lizzie. I haven't seen her since yesterday when she was in Daddy Warbucks' suite. I couldn't sleep last night either, tossing and turning with visions of them having a threesome.

I shouldn't have said all that stuff. I know she isn't the sort of girl to sleep around, at least I don't think she is. Even if she is, it's not for me to judge. Why couldn't she see I just wanted to spend time with her? I liked her. I still like her and can't get her out of my mind.

All I've thought about this evening since the sea became rough is how she is coping with her sea-sickness. After seeing her the other night with the storm, I wonder if she's the same again tonight. Even though it's much milder, I still worry.

After my shift, I make her some lemon tea and grab a packet of those ginger cookies from the restaurant. I knock on her cabin door and hear a shuffling.

"Hello?" She sounds groggy, like she's just waking up.

I hope I didn't wake her. She'll definitely be pissed with me.

"Lizzie. It's me."

"Ugh. What do you want?"

Fuck, she's still mad. Sure she is. "Elizabeth, please. Are you all right? I've brought a peace offering."

She opens the door, wearing her shorts and t-shirt that says 'thick thighs and pretty eyes'. Her hair is in a messy bun high on top of her head, and she doesn't have any makeup on, but she's never looked more beautiful.

"Hi, kitten." I hold the tray up a little, showing her the snacks.

"You can shove your peace offering up your arse." The door slams in my face and she yells, "I'd sooner be ill than take anything from you."

After last night, I deserve that. "I'm sorry, I'm so sorry. I know that doesn't mean much, but let me make it up to you."

I hear a sniffle on the other side of the door and my heart crushes like it's plummeted to the deepest depths of the ocean.

"You're just going to hurt me again. It's better to just let things be."

Hearing a wobble in her voice, I know she's crying and I need to hold her, comfort her. If only she'd let me. I set the tray down on the floor and rest my forehead against the door. "No Lizzie, it's not better this way. I won't leave us like this. It was wrong to say those things last night. I didn't mean any of it. I was hurt. You wouldn't listen to the truth and you thought the worst of me over the tour business."

"The truth is, you cancelled my trip like you were doing me a favour."

"The truth is, I went down to the dock to see if there were any spaces on the coach for me, but it was fully booked. When you didn't show, I actually thought you'd changed your mind. I told Roxy you probably weren't gonna come, but she wouldn't admit to that, as she could get in trouble if you put a complaint in for not waiting the allocated time."

My palms press flat against the door and I train my ear for any movement, but there's only the sound of silence. My heart travels further into the abyss, starved of oxygen, waiting for her to respond.

After waiting for what must be fifteen minutes, the door handle creaks down and opens. She stands sideways with flushed, wet cheeks.

I pick up the tray and enter her cabin. "I wasn't sure if you would have sea-sickness again, so I brought you some lemon tea and ginger cookies, just in case." With my trembling hands, I set the tray down on the table, hoping she will talk to me at least.

She throws her arms around me as I turn back around. Her shoulders shake as she sobs into my neck. My hands instantly rub her back, and I relax with her in my arms again.

"Lizzie." I glide my palms up her top and rub the bare skin on her back, feeling the warmth from her body that I've missed for the last two days.

"I've missed you," she cries, squeezing me tight. "And I've felt ill all evening."

I rub her back again. "Shh. It's okay. I'm here." I kiss

her cheek, getting a taste of her salty tears. "Lizzie, I'm sorry I was a jerk. I shouldn't have said anything to Roxy. But when you didn't show, I was hopeful you'd changed your mind and decided to spend the day with me."

She pulls away to look at me. Her eyes are like a Hawaiian waterfall, causing a dull ache in my lungs.

"No, I'm sorry." Tears drip from her swollen lips, and I wipe them away with my thumb.

"You have nothing to be sorry for. I was the jerk. I stepped over a line.

"I should have given you the benefit of the doubt. You were right. I had a better time with you. I was just upset that you were a little controlling. If I could do it all again, I would always choose you."

I smother her mouth. My tongue slips between her parted lips, dipping and whirling around hers. Coming back up for air, I cup her face. "I will always choose you." I peck her forehead, then her nose. "How are you feeling?"

"Terrible."

"Here, get in bed." I fluff her pillow and straighten her sheets. "I'll make you a fresh tea. This one's gone cold. Have you had any Dramamine?"

"Not since earlier."

The tablets are on her nightstand. I take two out of the packet and hand them to her, along with the packet of cookies.

"Thank you for this."

I snuggle next to her in the bed and kiss the side of her head above her ear. "Anything for you, kitten."

The smell of lemon fills the room as she sips her tea. "You hurt me last night."

"I know. I said I was sorry. Can we forget about it?" I take hold of her free hand in mine and interlace our fingers together, needing to be close to her.

"Yes. After I've told you something. I need to get it off my chest."

"Go on." I brace myself for round two, sensing a lecture.

"I've only ever slept with three people in my entire life." She blows into her drink and takes another sip.

My mouth drops open. That's not what I was expecting her to say. "Why are you telling me this? You don't have to explain yourself to me."

"I need you to know that I don't just sleep around, and I don't just sleep with anyone."

"So am I number four?"

She bites into her cookie and wipes the crumbs from her lips while crunching it down. "Number three," she mumbles.

I gently bump her shoulder and smile. "Third time lucky, hey?"

She giggles that cute giggle that makes my heart sing. It's nice to see her smiling again, even with a mouthful of cookie.

"I sort of knew that. I didn't mean any of that shit I said last night. But to be honest, I don't care how many people you slept with before me, as long as I'm the last." I realise what I've just said and know I won't be the last. We won't even be on the same continent after next week.

I could get out of my employment contract, but then I won't get my bonus. But what would I do in England? That isn't in my plan. But then, neither is she and yet here

I am, begging for her forgiveness. I know I shouldn't have told Roxy she wasn't coming, but I won't apologise for wanting to spend time with her. Although, I finally understand the phrase my grandfather used to say 'a happy wife is a happy life'. I lean back against the headboard with a curve on my lips, remembering my nonno's words of wisdom.

She smiles with hooded eyes, finishing her drink and cookies while snuggling into me. "I think the Dramamine is working. Will you stay with me tonight?"

"I'm not going anywhere."

CHAPTER Sixteen

LIZZIE

A WARM BREEZE swathes my skin. I inhale a deep breath and blink open my eyes to the bright light coming from the open patio doors. I turn to the side of me, but I'm alone in my bed. He said he would stay. I exhale, looking around the room for a note and pad over to the bathroom, clean my teeth, then flick the kettle on. It's still warm.

A shadow blocks out the sun. His silhouette is before me, leaning against the sliding door in his work trousers and nothing else.

"Morning, kitten. How are you feeling?" He walks over to me and wraps his arms around my waist. My skin breaks out in gooseflesh as his hands slip under my pyjama top and caress the bare skin of my back.

My face nuzzles into his warm chest. "I'm a little queasy still. I thought you'd left."

"I told you I wasn't going anywhere. Let me make you tea." He takes a cup and opens a sachet, then pours the boiled water into my mug.

We sit on the reclining chairs on the balcony with nothing in view except an expanse of sea, reaching the horizon. Water laps against the hull as we move at a steady pace and the ship's engine hums beneath us. The sun kisses the surface, illuminating the water like crystals dancing on the gentle waves.

"What time are you working today?" I sip my hot drink and close my eyes, feeling the rays on my face.

"I start at midday, and I finish at ten."

"That's a long shift."

"We can hang out this morning and after work if you like. Maybe I'll take you to the slots. You've been hanging around there long enough."

"I'd love that. I finally plucked up the courage to have a go, and they closed the casino."

"Yeah, no gambling allowed in Hawaii."

"Do you play?"

"Sometimes. I'm not actually allowed to play on the ship, but I do sometimes in LA. It's probably the only skill my old man ever taught me."

"Oh, does your dad play a lot?"

He huffs out a laugh. "You could say that. He's a compulsive gambler. One reason Ma and I never had a penny to our name."

I reach out my hand and take hold of his. "I'm sorry. Do you still see your dad?"

"Not if I can help it."

My heart aches for him. I know what it's like to not have your parents around.

"Shall we order breakfast? You might feel better when you've eaten something."

"Good idea. I'm starving. What do you like?"

"I'll have a full English. My ma cooked those for me on special occasions."

I walk back into the cabin, pick up the phone and dial

room service, ordering Zac's full English and scrambled eggs and toast for myself.

After placing the order, I return to the balcony and take a seat. "It will be about twenty minutes." I raise an eyebrow and smile.

He sits up straight in his seat. His eyes wide with a smirk playing on his lips. "Are you feeling a little better, then?"

I play with the hem of my pyjama shorts. "A little, but I think you could make me feel even better." With flushed cheeks, I look up through my lashes.

He stands, knocking the table. My drink topples over. I cry out and jerk back, but the warm tea splashes me, soaking into my pyjama shorts.

"Fuck. Lizzie, I'm sorry." He runs inside the cabin and returns with a towel. "I'm such an idiot. Are you okay?" He wipes my legs.

"Zac, I'm fine. It wasn't hot."

He straightens, pulls me from the chair and disappears into the cabin.

I hear the shower turn on, then a clink. I walk into the bathroom to see his belt and trousers in a puddle on the floor.

My eyes wander his slender body, settling on the swallow tattoo that soars as his chest rises and falls. He steps forward, closing the gap between us, and guides me into the small shower cubicle.

The water rains down and I lift my face, enjoying the warm drops on my skin.

"Can we both fit in here?"

"We will when you're pinned against the wall." He smirks and my core clenches, then his lips crush my mouth. My racing pulse drowns out the noise of the shower. His tongue darts between my parted lips and swirls, just like my head swirling from his touch. My skin is hyper-aware of every feathery stroke from his fingers as his hands roam my body.

Zac pulls off my top, then trails kisses down my neck. His lips trickle down to my breasts along with the rivulets. He tucks his fingers under the elastic of my shorts and pulls them off, letting them drop to the shower floor.

"Turn around." His voice is deep, rough, commanding, but his hand trembles as it glides down my stomach to the sensitive area between my thighs. My stomach flutters like a fish flapping its fins. Zac pushes me forward, forcing my breasts against the cool tiles, and I rest my palms against the shower wall.

"Spread your legs, kitten."

The throb between my thighs intensifies, and I widen my stance, pushing out my arse a little. He presses his erection between my cheeks and tugs at the bobble in my hair that's now wet and limp under the flow of water. Once he's untangled it from my hair, he runs his fingers through my curls and groans in my ear.

"Bend over for me."

I stick my arse out more and arch my back. My eyes close. I gasp as he pushes his length into my channel. My legs shake, and I slide my hands up and down the wall, trying to grab a hold of something, but there's nothing there, only the slippery tiles. One of his hands covers mine against the wall, holding them in place, and he pulls out and pushes in slowly, filling me to the hilt with the full length of him.

The hot water hitting my back adds to the pleasure. His fingers massage my bundle of nerves, and the pressure builds in my core. I turn to my head to see his face.

"Zac."

"Yes, kitten," he groans, tugging on my hair and pulling my head back so he can suck my neck.

His thrusting increases, and his groans turn to pants. My sex clenches around him. Blinding white lights flash before me, making everything hazy, but his face is crystal clear. How can anyone else ever compare to him? It's like tasting champagne, but then you have to settle for wine. I can't go back to my mundane life, not now I've tasted the stars.

Our bodies slow to a halt. I straighten my back, and he kisses my cheek. "Feeling better now?"

I let out a hum and a long breath, dipping my head back against his shoulder as the last few sparks fire in my centre.

There's a knock at the door. "Fuck." He steps out of the shower and wraps a towel around him. "You'll have to get that. If I'm caught in here with you. I'll get canned."

With shaky legs, I grab the robe from the hook in the bathroom and open the main cabin door. "Thank you."

I take the tray of food and place it on the bed, then lay on my side next to it. I pinch one of Zac's sausages and dip it into the beans on his plate.

He walks out of the bathroom with his trousers on. "Hey, are you eating my sausage?"

I giggle and dip the sausage in his beans again. "Sorry, but I couldn't resist your sausage."

"You're definitely feeling better, then?"

I nod, chewing on the juicy meat and lick the grease from my fingers. "I said you could make me feel better. Who said you could get dressed, anyway?"

"Who said you could have my sausage?"

My lip sticks out, and he leans forward. His biceps bulge as he cages me in and sucks on my pouty lip.

"What's the pout for? You want my other sausage, don't you?"

"Yes, but I also want you to myself all day, and you have to go to work soon."

He picks the second sausage from his plate and places it in front of my mouth. "You can have this sausage now and my big sausage tonight."

A giggle bursts from my lips. "And you say I'm the confident one."

"You give me an ego boost every time you scream my name, sweetheart. What can I say?" He winks, causing a flutter in my core.

I take a bite, then mumble. "You have the rest. I'll save myself for the big one again later."

He finishes the sausage and then tucks into the rest of his breakfast, adding a sachet of brown sauce. "Eat up before it gets cold."

The smell of my scrambled eggs makes my stomach growl, distracting me from him. Although watching him eat his full English is giving me food envy, and I wish I'd ordered a big breakfast for myself. I certainly worked up an appetite.

"I'm so glad you're here, Zac."

He swallows. "There's nowhere else I'd rather be." Leaning over the tray, he nuzzles my neck, then kisses my cheek, moving to my lips. I taste the sauce on his tongue and kiss him deeper.

AFTER BREAKFAST, we walk through the atrium, and I stop at a perfume shop. "I need to buy some presents. Do you mind shopping with me?"

"Not at all." Zac follows me into the store full of lotions and potions. The lights shine on the multitude of coloured bottles, lighting them up like jewels in Aladdin's cave.

The combination of sweet and floral aromas hit me as I make my way to the women's section.

"Are you after anything in particular?" Zac asks as I scan the shelves.

"I want a nice expensive perfume for my sister-in-law, Susie. She deserves a little luxury."

Zac picks up a pink bow shaped bottle, takes my arm and sprays the tester on my wrist. "This one reminds me of your garter tattoo."

The fruity fragrance lingers in the air, reminding me of sweets and summer. "This is so me. I love it. I'll buy that for myself." After scanning the shelves, I settle on Chanel for Susie, knowing I can't go wrong with a classic. "I need to choose one for my brother now. What's the one you wear?"

"Versace. It's over here." He points to the Versace stand in the middle of the store.

"I don't want it. I just want to make sure I don't buy the same."

His eyebrows squish together. "Don't you like it?"

"I love it. That's the problem. I don't want my brother reminding me of you." A giggle bursts from my lips and Zac swoops in and kisses me, making my pulse race and the usual fluttering of fish in my stomach that he always excites in me.

I pull away, glancing around to check we're alone. "Zac, someone could see you."

"I couldn't help it. You know every time you giggle I just want to eat you up. Anyhow, there's no one here." He kisses my nose before guiding me to the men's section. "This is a good aftershave for your brother, and one I don't own." He hands me a Dior box.

I pick up a small basket from a nearby stack. "That's perfect. Thank you."

The perfume shop opens up into the gift boutique where I grab a Stitch plush toy for my niece, a thin scarf for Susie, and a cap for Eddie. My eyes widen when I see a small Harry Potter gift section in the corner of the store and I dash over for a better look. Sadly, the clothing isn't in my size, which isn't a surprise, but I spot a nice silver pair of Hufflepuff cufflinks for Zac.

"Have you seen these? They would look good with your work shirts. You wear cufflinks, don't you?"

"Yeah, I had my eye on these until I saw how much they were." He lifts the price tag and shows me the cost. $80.00.

My eyes bulge at the price. "What are they, platinum?"

Zac huffs a laugh. "Must be."

"I'll get you them, if you like them."

"Don't worry about it, Lizzie. You don't have to get me anything."

"I want to. Let me buy you something to remember me by."

"I'll never forget you, kitten." He takes my face in his hand and softly kisses my lips.

"I'm still buying them for you." I pop them in the basket and his face lifts with a wide smile.

After adding the items to my on-board account, I leave them in the shop for a steward to take to my cabin—apart from Zac's gift, which he puts in his pocket. "I'll treasure these, Lizzie."

At the casino, I hover, watching an elderly couple play the slots, wondering how it all works.

Zac's hand rests on my bottom and squeezes my cheek through the thin cotton fabric of my daisy patterned sundress.

"Are you playing?" He nods to the slot machines in the casino as the elderly couple move elsewhere.

"I've never played the slots in my life. I don't know what to do."

"Do you want to play?"

"Yes." I hold up my small purse full of coins I changed a few days ago, but was too scared to use.

With his hand at the bottom of my back, Zac guides me towards a stool in front of the machine which the old dear was using. He gestures for me to sit down and takes my hand as I climb up onto it.

Once positioned, I'm the same height as him. He stands

behind me, his chin resting on my shoulder. I want to turn my head and kiss him, but I don't want to get him in trouble. My head is light and dizzy, like I'm trapped in a whirlpool.

I take a coin from the pouch and hand it to him.

"What's this?"

"My money."

"We're not playing coin pusher with quarters here. You can put notes in the slot machine, you know." He chuckles and shakes his head. "How much you got in that little pouch?"

"About a tenner's worth."

"That will last you all of about ten seconds." He reaches up and places the coin in the machine. "Okay, pull the lever."

It's stiff, but I give it a good yank and the bars spin on the screen.

A cherry, a bar and a blank.

I pop a coin in this time and yank the lever again.

7, 7, bar. Zac lets out a breath he was holding. "Hard luck. I thought you were gonna hit the jackpot then."

"Why? Is 7, 7, 7 the jackpot?"

"Yeah. Three cherries is the next best win."

I already feel like I've hit the jackpot with him. His palms glide from my waist over my hips and glide up and down my thighs. I pop another coin in the slot and pull the lever. Leaning back into him as the bristles on his jaw scratch my neck, followed by the softness of his lips caressing the soreness away as he lightly brushes against my skin.

A hum escapes me, and I close my eyes, uninterested in what the fruit machine says. I could get three in a row, and I don't think it could entice me away from his body right now.

"Have I told you how beautiful you look?"

"Not today." I pull the lever again.

He moves closer to me and presses his chest flush with my back. A hard bulge sticks into my arse cheek, and he groans in my ear. My breath hitches. My mind spins faster than the reels on the machine, and I shuffle in my seat, crossing my legs. The heat from the apex of my thighs rides up through my body like a wave building to a crescendo.

"You won," Zac shouts, making me jump.

Three lemons appear on the screen and the machine lights up. I was spiralling down the whirlpool and didn't even realise.

He squeezes my hand, pointing to the figure at the bottom of the screen that reads ten dollars. "You should quit now while you're ahead."

I pinch my eyebrows together. "I'm just warming up." Taking some coins from the pouch, I place several into the machine at once and the credits ding to life.

"Have you never gambled before?"

"Only with my heart." I'm gambling with that right now, and I can't stop myself. The odds aren't good, and it will all end in tears, but I need as much of Zac as I can get, even if it's for a few more days.

ZAC

SHE KEEPS POPPING her coins in. Each time she pulls the lever, she holds her breath. Her eyes sparkle with wonder, like a child's first time at an amusement park.

Her credits dwindle away until she has nothing left.

"I told you that money wouldn't last."

She pouts her lips. "I really thought I'd win something. I saw someone win over a hundred dollars on here last week."

"You should play at the beginning of the vacation. They pay out more to entice you back."

"Really?"

Her body slumps on the stool, and she lets out a long sigh. I want to see that bright smile again, so I pull my wallet from my slacks, open it up and pick out a ten-dollar bill; one of many tips I received last night.

I slide it into the slot machine, and it sucks it in, making a dinging sound on the machine. Lizzie glances at me and smiles. I nod at the lever. "Go on then."

She pulls it and watches the spinning reel. Two lemons and a cherry. She pulls the lever again and again, each time a different disappointment.

She hits a series of combinations and the machine flashes up with a bonus and a free spin. I tap the button, and she pulls the lever again. 7, 7, 7 flashes on the screen along with a musical jingle.

She claps her hands, yelling, "Oh, Zac. You've won."

My head spins around to see who heard. "You won, Lizzie. I can't play, remember?"

My heart races when the jackpot flashes up on the screen. Trust me to win the fucking jackpot, and I can't even cash it in. That's so typical. Just like I've met the girl of my dreams, but she lives on another continent. The story of my fucking life.

Lizzie jumps from the stool. "Shall I get an attendant?"

Before I speak, a crew member is here to verify the claim. "Is this your win, ma'am?"

Lizzie nods. "Yes." Her voice is almost a squeak as the smile on her face widens.

"You need to fill out some paperwork, and we'll have the money transferred into your account. Follow me."

Lizzie obeys the woman, and I tag along. She fills in the necessary paperwork, and the attendant sets up the transfer, telling her it will take several days to clear in her account.

We step out of the casino. Lizzie can't stop smiling. We head back to her room before I have to change for work. Once in her cabin, she throws her arms around my neck. Her lips press against mine. I open for her, allowing her tongue to flick in and out of my mouth. My body hums and vibrates like the ship's engine beneath us.

"Zac. You won." Her face gleams and she shakes my shoulders. "You should be happy. That's twenty-five thousand dollars towards your restaurant. Give me your bank details. I'll transfer it to you as soon as it's cleared."

My body stills with a slack jaw, not expecting her to offer that. "Thanks. You've no idea what that means. It's surreal." I blink, staring at this amazingly generous woman who continues to surprise me in all the best ways.

She kisses me again. "It's real Zac. Believe it. It's real."

I jot down my bank details on a cruise line notepad on her dressing table, still bewildered.

She pops it in her purse. "I'll see you later, won't I?"

I peck her lips. "I'll see you in the restaurant."

CHAPTER Seventeen

LIZZIE

I WAIT in the restaurant for Zac to finish his shift, sipping a glass of house wine. The last of the customers disperse and the staff clear away tables.

His warm breath rests on the back of my neck as his fingers sweep my hair to the side, sending a flurry of tingles down my spine. "I'm all done, kitten."

I stand and follow him to the bar.

"Josh, get us one of those bottles of that vintage champagne." He points to the stack of expensive drinks in the cooler.

"Zac, that's a hundred dollar bottle."

"Yeah, so?"

Josh rings up the till. "It's $119 ma'am. Room 6015 is it?" He looks between Zac and me to see who's paying. Zac nods.

"Wait, no. I'm not paying for a hundred dollar bottle of plonk."

Zac looks puzzled, pulling his eyebrows together. "You can afford it. We're celebrating."

I don't know how much on-board spending money I actually have left, and I need to be careful. I know I have the money he won today, but that's his money, and it hasn't even cleared yet.

"That's not the point. I can't drink that, with people going hungry in the world. I would sooner donate that money to charity and drink water."

"It didn't stop you drinking it the other night in Mr Nilsen's suite."

My thoughts scramble to think up an excuse. "That was before I knew how much it was."

"Josh, put that back and get us a bottle of sparkling water." They both chuckle at me.

I frown at Zac, then turn to Josh. "Just give us a bottle of house champagne."

Josh rings through the twenty-dollar bottle, and Zac pulls out a note.

"Hey, that's the first time you've ever paid for something." Josh takes his money and places it in the till.

"I know, right?" I flash Zac a smile.

"Come on." He takes the bottle along with two glasses, and I follow him outside the restaurant to the lift. He leads me to the top deck.

Once out of view, he takes my hand. We step outside onto the sports deck. The cool air hits me, but the feel of his hand in mine sends a warmth flooding through my veins.

We walk up some metal steps to what I think is called the crow's nest. "Are we allowed up here?" Various antennas are attached to the mast at the top, making it all look rather high tech and official.

"No, but there are no cameras here." He pulls out a

blanket that is tucked away in the corner. "Do you bring all the girls here?"

"No, you're the first. I brought the blanket from my room earlier." He lays it on the floor and sits down, peeling the foil from the champagne.

"Oh, I almost forgot. I found my cheque book in my hand luggage. Here." I pull the cheque I wrote earlier from my bag and hand it to Zac. "This may be easier to transfer your money. I'm struggling to get a signal to my banking app while we're at sea."

He takes the cheque and slips it into his trouser pocket. "Thanks."

I cuddle up next to him, holding my glass, then flinch when the cork pops, and flies into the air. "So, are we celebrating your win?"

He smiles. "That and us." Our glasses clink together and I take a sip.

"There won't be any *us* in a few days." I look down and pick at the frayed blanket. "We're like two passing ships."

He lifts my chin. "You're not a ship, Lizzie. You're a shooting star, lighting up my life for just a moment."

I'm lost for words. That's probably the most beautiful thing anyone's ever said to me. I close my eyes to hide the teary film of happiness forming.

Zac's warm lips press against my forehead. "Do you want there to be an *us* after your vacation?"

My eyes open, along with my heart. Could he really want to see me again? "Yes."

"We'll figure something out." He pecks my lips.

"Zac." My breath catches in my throat.

"If I wasn't tied into a contract on this ship, I would move to England with you."

I freeze. My mouth gapes. "You would?"

"In a heartbeat. You could get me a job working at that bar you own."

He thinks I own it? "I don't own a bar."

"Sorry, I thought you said you did."

My head shakes. "I managed a bar. I mean, I'm a bar manager."

"We can stay in touch until my contract's up in nine months."

"Please don't say things you don't mean. I couldn't take another heartbreak."

"I mean it, kitten. Now drink your champagne." He winks at me, and his cheesy grin is present again.

"How did I get so lucky?"

"I'm the lucky one, Lizzie." His lips brush mine again, and I'm lost at sea underneath a blanket of stars in the middle of the ocean; a world away from reality.

I glance upwards to a bright light blasting across the night sky. "Was that a shooting star?"

Zac takes my glass from me and places it next to his on the deck, then lies on his back, pulling me down to lie beside him. We stare up at the constellations.

"There's another, look." He points up at another bright light travelling through the heavens. "I used to do this with my ma when I was a kid."

"Tell me about your mum."

"Her name's Lillian. She grew up in England, moved to LA to pursue an acting career, and between jobs she waited tables at my nonno's restaurant. That's how she met my pa. One thing led to another, and she had me. Pa wouldn't marry her. He took off for a while, so my grandparents took us in. Her career was over, and she waited tables for the rest of her life."

"That's really sad."

"My pa only turned up when he wanted money. When my nonno died suddenly of a heart attack, not long after my nan passed away, there was no will. Pa sold the restaurant and moved to Las Vegas. I was just a teenager. That's when money was really tight, but Ma always make sure I had food in my belly. She'd tell me she'd eaten, but I knew she hadn't."

I kiss his cheek. "That must have been really hard."

"It was, but once I started modelling, I made sure Ma didn't want for anything. You remind me of her."

"Really?"

He chuckles. "Not in looks. That would be weird. You have the same English humour and kind heart."

"You have a kind heart, too. That must be who you get it from."

"She would love you."

"I'd love to meet her. She sounds like an amazing woman."

"She was."

"Was?" My eyebrows pull together, and I roll on my side to look at Zac.

"She died a few years ago. Cancer. That's when I left LA and started working on the cruise ships. I needed an escape." His eyes glisten, reflecting the moon.

"Zac, I'm so sorry." My chest tightens, and my throat is scratchy. I know how he feels and I wouldn't wish that

ZAC

My vision blurs, gazing into her weeping eyes. A tear rolls off my temple, but I smile, thinking of Ma. I miss her. Whenever I look up at the sky, I'm reminded of her.

"I've never told anyone about my family before. Josh knows. We grew up together. He's like a brother to me. He helped me get my first cruise job. And this one. It's becoming a habit. He always has my back."

She softly kisses my lips as if she can kiss the pain away. Her mouth moves to my temple, kissing away my tears before snuggling into my chest. Her fingertips trace the scars on my arm like tracing the stars in the sky putting the dots together.

"My parents died in a car crash," she whispers.

I hold my breath. My stomach hardens, and I squeeze her tight. "Kitten." I kiss the top of her head as it rests on my chest. "Do you want to talk about it?"

"I was eighteen. I had just started working at the bar part-time while I finished college, and Dwayne took me in. My brother was at uni. I was really down and never finished my business studies. I should have had therapy, but I didn't want to talk about it with anyone."

She trembles in my arms, and I stroke the hair from her neck.

"It's okay, I'm here. You can talk to me whenever you like, and I'll listen."

She lets out a long breath. "I think that's why I put up with Dwayne for so long. Other than my brother, he was all I had."

"You have me now." I kiss her head again and glide my hand up and down her spine. "Another shooting star, look."

She rolls back onto her back, staring up at the sky. I take hold of her hand and interlace our fingers.

"Do you see that cluster of stars?" I point to the sky. "Like a square, with three legs."

"Yes, I see it."

"That's Pegasus. She's a guide for our souls to leave the physical world and enter the spirit realm where we can soar without limits of time or space. So when you look up into the sky, know that your parents are free and soaring over the oceans and always with you."

"I never knew you were so deep."

I glance at her beautiful face. She's staring up at the sky in total wonder, with her bright eyes twinkling like the stars above.

"Zac, it's so beautiful."

I lean up on my elbow and hover over her. My fingers sweep away the hair from her face, then trail the curve of her cleavage. "The view from here is pretty spectacular, too."

My heart is ready to burst like a supernova. Gazing into her eyes has sparks firing inside my body like shooting stars travelling straight to my dick. She breathes out a trembled breath matching my own quivering lungs.

There are so many things I want to tell her, but I know it's too soon.

"Kiss me," she whispers.

I crash my lips to hers. Heat pulses through my body like an asteroid entering the earth's atmosphere.

My body shakes as I hold my weight above her. "I can't believe I only have three more days with you."

"Let's make them memorable."

CHAPTER
Eighteen

LIZZIE

LYING BY THE POOL, the sun's rays burn into my flesh. Beads of moisture bubble on the surface, and I welcome the cool breeze rolling off the water. Zac is working behind the pool bar this afternoon, hence why I'm hanging out here. Each time he walks by, he flashes me a smile and a wink. I dip my sunglasses, getting a good look at his toned arse.

"Excuse me, sir."

He walks over. "Yes, ma'am."

"Can I have another one of those cocktails, please?"

"Certainly ma'am. Anything else."

"A kiss wouldn't go a miss." The corner of my mouth curls upwards.

He leans down and whispers in my ear, "I'll give you more than a kiss, sweetheart. Meet me in the changing room in five minutes."

With my racing heart I scramble from the sun lounger to my feet and dab the moisture from my face with my towel, then over my plump stomach that's on show between my floral bikini, wiping the sweat away from my sun-kissed skin.

I walk to the small changing room and close the door

behind me. The facility is spacious, with a luxurious marble floor and sparkling fixtures and fittings. Like the rest of the ship, they've spared no expense, even down to the tiny details.

A knock sounds from the door. I open it and Zac pushes in quickly, locking the door behind him. He turns around and takes my face in his hands, bringing his lips to mine.

"Do you know how much my dick throbs seeing you lying there in this bikini?"

"No, tell me." I reach down and palm his erection over his trousers.

He spins us around, pinning me against the door, dipping his tongue in my mouth and pressing his hard body against my breasts.

His hand delves into my bottoms. "I've had a hard-on all morning because of you," he growls, slipping his nimble fingers into my wet heat, and circling my bundle of nerves with his thumb. "Just thinking about this wet pussy of yours."

"You could have had me this morning if you hadn't rushed off."

"I had to shower and change for work, you know that."

"I wish you'd woken me. I was disappointed to wake up alone."

"Didn't you see enough of me last night? I thought you needed your sleep."

My legs teeter beneath me, trembling with every flick of his agile finger.

I unbuckle the belt to his trousers and slip my hand down under the fabric of his boxer shorts. He groans, then sucks under my ear, sending tingles through my body, travelling straight to my centre.

I grip his full length in my hand and with each movement back and forth, his massaging fingers flicker faster inside me and his thumb presses firmly against my bud. My eyes close as the pressure builds in my stomach.

His hand wraps around my throat. "Look at me. You know the drill by now, kitten."

I stare into his fluorescent green eyes that are hotter than a jalapeño right now. He holds my throat, keeping my head in place. My breath is heavy, my pulse races faster than a speedboat as he rubs his thumb over me again and again at a steady rhythm.

My head swims as my walls clench. I automatically close my eyes as the orgasm crashes over me in a wave of pleasure. His thumb presses against the throbbing pulse in my neck, making my eyes flick open and another wave of pleasure washes over me.

His fingers slow along with my breathing. Soft moans escape my lips as my head spins in a whirlpool, drowning in this ecstasy he's giving me. I had stopped moving my hand down his length, overcome with euphoria. He removes his hand from my throat and places it over mine, forcing my hand up and down his erection. He sets the pace, fast and hard, and squeezes over my hand.

He pulls my hair, forcing my head back so he can have access to my neck, and places his hot lips there, sucking on my skin, no doubt marking my flesh with his mouth.

A knock on the door vibrates against my back, and I hold my breath.

Zac doesn't seem affected and continues to nibble at my neck.

Another knock.

"Just give me five minutes," I shout, hoping they'll go elsewhere.

Zac smirks. "Five minutes?"

"Yes, you're nearly done, aren't you?"

"I will be when you suck it."

My mouth drops open.

"You'll need to open a little wider than that, sweetheart." He smiles with hooded eyes, and I drop to my knees, hoping to wipe that cocky smirk from his face when he loses all control.

His palms rest against the door and his head tilts, watching me as I take his erection in my hand and lick at the salty tip. His hips rock steadily, pushing his dick in and out of my mouth. With each movement, he hits the back of my throat.

Another knock at the door.

Zac growls. "In a minute."

His thrusts get faster. He grips my hair, keeping my head in place while he does all the work. Each time he pushes in, the tip hits the back of my throat, making me gag, and my eyes water.

"Lizzie," he groans.

Warm liquid fills my mouth, and I swallow before I gag again.

With his shaky legs, he slows the rocking of his hips, catching his breath. He releases my hair and presses both palms against the door. I stand between his arms, caged by his biceps and he rests his forehead against mine, kissing my nose.

His thumb swipes the corner of my mouth. "You missed some."

I lick the saltiness from his pad before wetting my lips.

He smirks. "I always knew you had a big mouth."

I tut and roll my eyes, but can't stop smiling. "Almost as big as yours."

He presses his lips to mine in a long, searing kiss. "I best get back to work."

"You better. I'm still waiting for my cocktail."

"You just had your cock-tail." He chuckles.

I giggle along with him. "It's thirsty work, all that saltiness."

"One cocktail coming right up." He pecks my lips again and opens the door, giving me a wink as he walks away.

I wait in the changing area a few minutes before exiting myself.

"Elizabeth, isn't it?"

I turn around to see a petite blonde girl walking behind me. She stops.

"Yes, can I help you?"

"No, but I can help you."

"How?" I squish my eyebrows together and look down at her tiny frame. Perfect skin, hair, teeth, and body.

"He's using you."

"Excuse me?"

"Zac. He's using you for what he can get. It's what he does. I've been working on cruise ships with him for over a year now. He finds the richest women, who are single or vulnerable, and he fleeces them for all he can get."

My heart rate picks up a few knots. I fold my arms across my stomach. "But I'm not rich." I hold my breath. My heartbeat thrums in my ears as the blood rushes to my head. He thinks I'm wealthy. Has he been playing me all along? I shake my head. No, he wouldn't do that. Would he? "Why are you telling me this?"

"I just don't like seeing girls get hurt. It's clear you're falling for him. I saw how you looked at him earlier when he walked by."

"Nothing's going on between us."

"Sure. Just be careful he doesn't screw you over."

With a tightness in my lungs, I scan the pool area for Zac and watch as he approaches an older woman at the far end of the pool. He's carrying an ice bucket housing a bottle of champagne and a glass flute in his hand. The woman bites her lip, tugs on his waistcoat, bringing him close to her as he places the champagne bucket on the small table next to her sun lounger. She whispers something while pulling money from her bag, and tucks it into his trousers like you would a stripper.

My stomach twists, forcing acid to rise in my throat.

"See. I told you he has form. I wonder what he's done to earn that wad of cash." The blonde says next to me.

I glance at her, then back to Zac, who winks as he walks away, adjusting himself and counts the notes he just pulled from his trousers. How did I never notice this before? I have been blind. After everything I've been through with Dwayne, and this guy has been flirting with every Tom, Dick and Harry, or should I say, Sue, Deb and Sally.

Bile fills my mouth, along with his cum I swallowed a moment ago. I dash back into the changing room and retch down the sink, bringing up everything, including my continental breakfast.

A sticky sweat coats my skin, but I'm no longer hot. My body shivers, and I retch again, until there's nothing left.

A knock on the door. "Hey, are you all right in there?" The blonde girl shouts through the door. My body shakes and retches again. I stand and look at my pale face in the ornate mirror. Patting myself with a wet paper towel, how could I let myself fall for him? I didn't even realise how much I have fallen for him until now.

It's like Dwayne all over again. I will never forget the day I walked into the beer cellar to see him burying his dick into the twenty-year-old barmaid. At least Zac hasn't traded me in for a younger model. I gasp and cover my mouth. He likes older women because they have money. That's why he's been seeing me. The acid burns my throat. Turning the tap on, I place my mouth under the running water and gulp down the cold liquid. Everything makes sense now. He was always putting drinks on my tab, like I'm loaded or something. Plus, he thought I owned the bar I used to work at.

"Are you okay?" The girl calls again.

I open the door. "Does he do this with all the guests?"

She pulls her eyebrows together. "No, only the ones he thinks will tip well. The slightly older ones mainly."

I push past her with weak knees and walk to my sun lounger to grab my bag. I need to get away from him. As I approach, he's talking to another woman. This one looks like she's in her fifties. His fingers trickle down her arm, and I see flashes in my vision.

Memories of Dwayne spiral through my head. I watched him show that girl more affection in one shag than he showed me in all the years we were together.

I throw my beach bag on my shoulder and walk towards the elevator.

"Lizzie."

I ignore him. Pressing my lips together, I breathe heavily through my nostrils as I pick up speed to the double doors.

"Lizzie, are you all right?" He grabs my arm, pulling me back.

I glare at him and yank my arm free.

"What's wrong?"

I press the button for the elevator.

"Lizzie, talk to me."

"Go and talk to your sugar mummies or whatever it is you call them."

He snorts out a laugh. "What the fuck are you talking about?"

The lift pings open. I step into it and glare at him before the doors close. He's staring back with his mouth gaping. Bastard.

ZAC

Fuck. What's got into her? I think back to the changing room. I'm sure she was smiling after I left. When I turn around, Jessica is standing there with a smirk on her face.

I stomp over. She turns to walk away.

"What the fuck did you say to her?" I shout.

"Nothing, that wasn't the truth." She continues walking.

"Splitting us up isn't going to make me want you again?"

She turns around. "So you admit you're a couple, then?"

"We were until you started meddling. What have you said?"

"Nothing. I didn't have to say anything. She saw you up to your usual tricks with that woman." Jessica laughs wildly.

My stomach sinks like an anchor dropping to the ocean floor with a thud, churning up the seabed.

Jessica turns around and walks away. My chest pounds thinking of my kitten being upset with me again. I wasn't doing anything I don't normally do. I hate that I have to flirt, but it's kinda part of the job description. In the three years I've been doing this gig, she's the first guest I've ever slept with.

"Makani, I'm taking a break," I yell across the pool, making my way to the elevator. I can't bear it when she's mad at me. We only have today and tomorrow left, and I'll be damned if I'm spending them apart.

The car dings when it reaches her floor. I step out and make my way down the corridor. Wiping my sweaty palms on my slacks, I think about what to say. Her face had turned white like when she was seasick. I just want to look after her. She may be older, but I feel she needs someone to look out for her.

I rasp my knuckles on the door. "Lizzie."

"Go away."

"I'm not going anywhere until you talk to me."

"Well, you'll have a long wait, then."

"If you don't open this door, I'll call Koa and get a universal key card."

"And I'll call security and have you removed."

"Open the fucking door, Elizabeth."

She flings it open. Her hands are in tight fists digging into her hips, and her cheeks are stained with tears. "Why? So you can play me again, like your other cougars. I guess the apple doesn't fall far from the tree."

"I'm just being friendly. You know that."

"Yes, friendly to get a good tip. Well, you can stop being friendly with me because I'm broke."

I huff. "I think me and you have different ideas of being broke, sweetheart."

"What's that supposed to mean?"

"It means that my version of broke is a little different from yours."

"You think I don't know what it's like to not know where your next meal is coming from, or where you're going to sleep? You're not the only one that's suffered."

"Well, princess, if you're ever that hard up, you could always sell your Louis Vuitton luggage. And you've been spending on board like your money is burning a hole in your pocket. I'd hardly call that broke."

Another burst of fresh tears fall down her cheek. "It's

fake. It cost me fifty quid off the market a few years ago. And this." She waves her hand around the luxurious cabin. "This was a competition I won. It came with fifteen-hundred dollars on-board spending money which I have to spend or I lose it. I can't draw it out in cash." Her hand trembles as she wipes the tears from her face. I step closer to hug her, but she pushes me away.

"When Dwayne cheated on me, I left him, his apartment, and my job. I moved into my brother's spare room. The only thing I own is my old Ford Fiesta that's worth about five-hundred quid."

I close my mouth. She's actually broke. "Why didn't you say anything?"

"It's not something I want advertised. I'm sorry you wasted your time with me when you could have been screwing a millionairess."

"I've never asked you for a cent. You think I care about how much money you have?"

"Of course you do. I've seen you with my own eyes. It all makes sense now. You're always flirting with the old tarts. You even have a picture of one in your cabin. She must have been really wealthy for you to keep a picture of that old slapper."

I clench my jaw, then my fist. "I can't believe you said that." My lungs gasp for air as I breathe in deep, heavy breaths. "Vicious doesn't look good on you, sweetheart." I spit the words at her.

She gasps, but at least she's stopped talking. Her eyes turn to grey like when the sun's rays are hidden from the sea.

Reaching into my slacks pocket, I pull out my wallet and the cheque she wrote me.

"This is how much I care about your fucking money." I tear the cheque in half. "Keep it. Sounds like you need it more than me." I stomp out of the cabin. There's a ringing in my ears and black spots in my vision. I can't get her words out of my head. They keep playing over and over again.

Does she not know me at all? How could she think I was using her for money? Maybe I was after a few tips in the beginning, but that was before I got to know her. I knew there was something different about her from our very first encounter. Did I ever know her? I guess I didn't know her like I thought I did. The Lizzie I fell in love with would never have said all those hurtful things to me.

My heart weighs heavy in my chest, making it difficult to breathe. The last place I want to go is back to the pool bar, but I have another two hours left of my shift. To think, I swapped with Sally so I could spend the evening with her. That's not going to happen now.

CHAPTER Nineteen

LIZZIE

MY THROAT PRICKLES as tears stream down my face. I've never seen him so angry or hurt. But I'm hurt. I won't be made a fool of again. I pick the two halves of the cheque up and place them in my bin. What a mess. I shouldn't be this upset. I wouldn't have seen him after the holiday, anyway.

I vowed I would never cry over a man again, and here I am bawling my eyes out. Although I tell myself it's not so much about him but more feeling sorry for my situation. As much as I love my brother and his wife, living in their spare room with no money or job was never my life's ambition. It could be worse, and I could be on the streets, I suppose.

I dry my tears and take a shower, washing the sun cream from my body and the feel of Zac from my skin. After drying, I throw on my pyjamas, I can't face going out tonight or bumping into him. Perusing the menu, I order room service. I never did get that cocktail. Somehow I'm just not in the mood now, and I order a thick strawberry milkshake and a selection of desserts, skipping the main meal. I flick on the tv to see what movies are available and flop on the bed.

An hour later, a knock at the door causes my heart to stall, thinking it could be Zac.

"Room service." An unfamiliar voice calls out.

I relax and open the door to see his friend, Josh. "Ma'am." He walks into the cabin and places the tray of desserts on the table, along with my milkshake. "Will that be all, ma'am?"

"That's everything, thank you."

He walks out of the room and turns to face me before I close the door. "Zac's in the crew bar if you want to apologise."

"Apologise?" I pinch my eyebrows together. "Me. Apologise? I think he's the one that needs to apologise. I've done nothing wrong. Unless you mean letting him think I'm rich, then that's his own fault for being shallow."

"You called his mother a whore."

I flinch my head back. "No, I didn't. I haven't even mentioned his mother."

I cover my mouth with my hands. Holding my breath, my eyes grow wide and sting with prickling tears. "The woman in the picture is his mother?"

Josh nods. "He was pretty upset when I saw him."

A lump grows in my throat, and I choke out the words. "I'm sorry."

"You need to tell him that, not me. And for the record, I think he genuinely liked you. He may flirt, but I've never known him take things this far, if you know what I mean."

Josh walks down the corridor, and I close the cabin door. The cakes look so pretty garnished with fruit and chocolate sauce, but I'm not hungry anymore. My stomach sinks like a ship sinking to the depths of despair. I have to apologise.

I change into a casual summer dress that I wore a few days ago, put a little mascara and lippy on, and make my way to the stairs. I sneak through the staff door and delve deeper into the ship's hull to the crew bar. The disinfectant smell becomes stronger the further down I go.

The dark, dingy room seems gloomier than ever. Or is that just my mood? I scan all the corners for Zac but don't see him. The bartender asks what I would like, and I ask for a wine. May as well get shit-faced while I'm here, and drown my sorrows. "Have you seen Zac?"

The bartender points to the left, but all I see is a blonde in a glitzy silver dress straddling some guy, snogging his face off. My breath stalls. That's the blonde from today and no, no, no. Zac.

Tears threaten my eyes, and before I can even sip my drink, the glass slips through my fingers. There's a clatter as it hits the floor. All eyes turn to me. The liquid splashes my bare legs and shards of broken glass scratch at my skin.

The blonde smirks with her smeared lipstick. My body freezes. I'm screaming inside and desperate to move, but my legs won't conform. Zac's gaze meets mine. His eyes are a dull shade of sage, even with the black light shining on him from the bar. Lifeless and still, he looks away, as if disgusted by my presence. What was I thinking? My legs finally break out of the statue pose and dart to the door. They take me up the stairs as fast as they can go until I reach the top and push through the doors onto the starboard side.

Gasping for breath, I cling onto the railing and inhale the sea air as the wind whips at my cheeks. Has he been seeing her the whole time? I recognise her now in that silver dress. She's one of the dancers from the show. Of course, he would be seeing her. Why wouldn't he? She's young, slim, beautiful. She's probably flexible too, the lucky sod.

I never even got to taste my drink. I'm dying of thirst. My throat has never been so dry. Then I remember the milkshake back in my room. My head is dizzy, but I haven't eaten since breakfast.

Back at the cabin, I slip off my shoes, and with a warm flannel, I wipe a trickle of dry blood that's stained my leg. Once changed into my pyjamas, the TV's back on and I curl into bed with my desserts and milkshake that's gone sour, like my relationship with Zac. The only thing left to go wrong now is if this boat sinks. And the way my heart feels at the moment, I would go down with this ship.

ZAC

GLASS SHATTERS ON THE FLOOR, causing me to look up. I suck in a breath when I see her standing there with her eyes locked on me. I try to stand, but something has me pinned in my seat. Fuck. Jessica. I'm seeing three of her straddled on top of me. No wonder I can't move. Have I drunk that much? I focus on the middle one. "Get the fuck off me."

"You weren't saying that a minute ago."

"I wasn't even conscious a minute ago."

Her smeared pink lips curl up in one corner. She looks like the joker in that film. I huff, then look back at my Lizzie. She runs out of the room, but it's like I'm watching it happen in slow motion. I pick Jessica up off my lap and seat her in the chair next to me.

"You're not seriously going to run back to Miss Piggy, are you?"

"Fuck off, Jess." I stumble through the bar. I can't see where she went. Did I even see her? Am I hallucinating? How much have I drank? I press the buttons on the lift, watching them light up like a Christmas tree. Stopping on every floor on the way to hers, I look into the spinning mirror on one wall of the elevator and see my face covered in pink lipstick. My Lizzie doesn't wear pink. She wears red. I spit on my sleeve and try to wipe it off. This won't go down well. Arriving on her deck, I walk down her corridor and bump into Josh, then bounce against the wall.

"Zac. What the fuck happened to you?"

"I've been attacked by Jessica." My words come out slurry. "She's like one of those spiders that eats her mate." I chuckle, but have no clue why.

"Where are you going?"

"I'm going to sort things out with my kitten." My vision blurs. Everything is doubled.

"You can't let her see you like this. She'll never talk to you again."

Josh hooks an arm under mine. I stumble back into the lift.

"Lizzie's room is that way." I point to the door, then

spin and point in the other direction, not actually knowing which way her room is.

"Sleep it off. You can see your lady-luck tomorrow."

MY HEAD POUNDS like a dingy being thrashed about in rough wind. Koa's alarm rings out and I roll over, pulling the pillow over my ears. It must be morning, even though you can never tell in this cabin with no natural light. It could be the middle of the night or afternoon and I wouldn't know. With the hangover from hell, I don't care either.

I'm not at work until this afternoon, and I contemplate staying in bed all day.

Koa climbs out from the bottom bunk. He taps the side of my bars. "You awake?"

I grunt. "No."

"I heard things got messy last night."

"Ah fuck. How bad was it?"

"You threw up in the bathroom and the room smelt of piss when I came back. Have you wet yourself?"

"Fuck off. I wasn't that bad."

Koa laughs. "You messed up with that girl you've been seeing, though. Josh says she ordered a tray of desserts and milkshakes and she was in her pyjamas early."

"Yeah, I don't want to talk to her or see her again, anyway. I'll be glad when she gets off this fucking boat. All she's done is cause grief."

"Isn't that what all women do?" He chuckles.

I roll over and close my eyes. "Turn the light out when you're done. I'm going back to sleep."

I sigh, knowing none of what I said is true. She's gotten under my skin, and I need to sort this mess out before she leaves tomorrow, but my head hurts. I need to ditch the hangover so I can grovel at her feet.

When I eventually rise, I check my phone to see a text summoning me to the office. For fuck's sake. I already feel like shit. Management doesn't need to slap me on the wrist and tell me not to drink again. I doubt I'll drink for a while.

After dressing in my uniform, I walk to the office and knock on the door.

"Come in."

I enter and the manager gestures for me to take a seat. She pushes her spectacles up the bridge of her nose and shuffles some paperwork, busying herself. All for effect, I'm sure.

"Look, I had a few drinks yesterday and then slept it off. Nothing happened."

She raises an eyebrow. "It's been brought to my attention that you have been fraternising with the guests."

"That's a lie." I huff.

"We have evidence that we cannot overlook." She continues to speak, but all I hear is my blood pumping as rage bubbles under my skin. Can the last two days actually get any worse? She turns her laptop around with a view of the changing room door from the pool deck. The video plays and I see Lizzie enter and I follow.

My heart pounds like the sea crashing against the ship on a stormy night. Fuck. This is worse than when my modelling contracts dried up. At least I had somewhere to live back then. A million things go through my head.

She closes the laptop case with a thud, jerking me back to the present. "We have no choice but to let you go."

"This is a misunderstanding. I went in there…to help her. She'd cut herself." My brain fumbles to make a sentence.

The manager tilts her head and sighs. "That's not what she said, Zac. This isn't the first time something like this has happened."

I clench my fists into tight balls and stand. "Yes, it is. What happened on the last ship was *her* coming onto *me*, and *me* turning *her* down. It's why there was a complaint by my ex-girlfriend. But the husband wouldn't believe it and obviously took his wife's side. That's why I was fired. This…" I wave my hand in the air. "This is a completely different situation."

She sighs, taking off her glasses. "It doesn't matter, Zac. The evidence backs up the claims and we're left with no other choice. I'm sorry. Please hand in your uniform. You won't be needing it again, but we will allow you to stay on board until we dock back in LA tomorrow."

She dismisses me. My stomach is in knots. I head up to the deck to get some fresh air, seeing as I won't be needed at work. My lungs feel like they're being strangled by my intestines.

Taking in several deep breaths, I inhale the grimy stench of the dock. I had lost track of where we were, but I recognise the Mexican port.

Walking down the promenade, I see Lizzie meandering towards me. Just as I was calming down, my mouth fills with a bitter taste and I flare my nostrils. She stops in front of me, biting on the inside of her mouth.

"I know you were upset with me, but I never thought you were this vindictive."

Her eyes glisten and bulge like the sea swelling before a tsunami. "I'm sorry, Zac. I never meant to say what I said."

"It's too late now. Looks like we're both jobless and homeless."

She steps closer. "What do you mean?"

"They fired me." I wave my hand in front of me, forcing her to step back. "Because of you, I got fired."

She opens her mouth, her eyes filling up with regret. "I'm so sorry."

"Save it for someone who gives a shit. If I never see you again, it will be too soon." I barge past her, knocking her shoulder as I storm by. I can't believe she actually got me fired.

CHAPTER Twenty

LIZZIE

I WALK BACK to my cabin with tears in my eyes. I never wanted him to get fired. Someone must have seen us. I gasp, hoping there weren't any cameras outside the changing room yesterday. Or on the roof when we were looking at the stars. My chest aches with guilt. I close the door to my cabin and lean back against it. My shoulders slump and my body slides to the floor in a puddle. Bringing my knees up as far as I can, I hug myself and allow the tears to fall. Tears for him and tears for my miserable life.

I have twenty-five thousand dollars sitting in my bank account that's not even mine. I don't want to keep his money. He will need it more than ever now. At least I have my brother to go back to. I pull my phone from my bag and connect to my banking. The signal is stronger now we're in port.

With the money cleared this morning, I've never been so wealthy. A shame it isn't mine, just like this life isn't mine. I thought I could pretend to be someone else for a while, but I wish I'd just been myself. He never would have looked twice at me then, and he could have kept his job and I could have kept what pieces of my heart I had left, instead of it scattered to the wind.

I rummage through my purse for the bit of paper Zac wrote his bank details on before I wrote him a cheque. Typing in the account number and sort code, I transfer £18,858 British pounds to Zac's account, leaving me with the £36 and 51p I had before I came here.

Using the cruise notepad and pen on the dressing table, I write him a note.

Dear Zac,

I'm sorry you were fired because of me. I wouldn't wish being homeless on anyone no matter how much I hate them. But I never hated you. I was falling in love with you.

I have transferred the money you won into your bank account so you can use it until you find another job. Maybe put it towards that Italian restaurant you've always dreamed of.

Thank you for giving me the best holiday of my life, even though I feel like it's also the worst. I had no idea the photo in your room was your mum. Please forgive me. I know how much she meant to you. I should have known better.

I wish you all the luck in the world.
Love Lizzie

A tear drops on the paper before I even know I'm crying. With the fabric of my dress, I dab under my eyes and wipe my cheeks. I miss him. The scent of pine trees reminding me of home, and the way he took care of me when I was sick. Nobody other than my parents has ever taken care of me like that. The way he made me feel sexy, confident and beautiful with just one look. I know he's a flirt. Maybe I should have let him explain himself after the pool incident instead of flying off the handle? Dwayne messed me up big time. I wonder if I'd have been more understanding, had I not been hurt before.

Although Zac should have known better than to flirt with every woman in a bikini? Am I at fault or him? I don't even know anymore. Maybe it's a bit of both. I know I said some things I shouldn't, which I'm so regretful for.

After folding the letter in half, I pop it in an envelope that's left in the room for tips and place it in my bag to hand in at reception the next time I'm passing. At least I'll feel better, knowing he has some money and won't be homeless.

ZAC

THE FAMILIAR LA cityscape stretches before me, when I peer out of the porthole on my way to grab breakfast. May as well make the most of the free food before departing.

I spent all day yesterday calling other cruise lines, but none have come back to me with any job offers as yet. I wish I'd kept that cheque now, but it sounded like Lizzie needed that money more than me. At least I have my wages and tips that I've saved. I'll be okay for a while until another job comes along.

With heavy limbs, I select a few continental breakfast items to take back to the cabin while I pack. I stare at the bread as it disappears under the grill, thinking where I'm going to stay tonight. As a last resort, I could always go and stay with my pa. I sigh, taking the toast and pastries back to my room.

Once all my shit is packed, I walk down the corridor with everything I own in this world packed into my suitcase. Including the cufflinks she bought me. Even though I'm angry and hurt, I can't seem to part with them.

Makani walks by with a smile on his face and a wad of cash, reminding me to check at the desk for any tips that may have been left for me.

Myka stands from behind reception. "Zac, I have a few things for you." She hands me some envelopes.

"Thanks."

I walk back down the corridor to the crew lounge, and slump into one of the chairs while I wait for Josh and Koa so I can say my goodbyes. Setting my suitcase on the floor, I prop my feet up, using it as a footstool, then open the envelopes. One has a fifty dollar bill and the other has a twenty. Another, two-hundred dollars.

The next one is a written note. My heart races as I read her letter. I thought she was the one that got me canned, but this letter reads differently. Have I made a mistake? Fuck. I check my banking on my phone and sure enough the money is pending in my account. Why would she do this? She needed that money.

Jessica walks through the lounge in last night's

clothing. "Awe, looks like your grave digging days are over." She laughs and points to my suitcase. "What a shame I won't see you again."

"It was you, wasn't it?"

"I don't know what you're talking about."

I grip her arm. "Why, Jess?"

"Let go of me. I'm not yours to manhandle anymore. You didn't want me. Run back to Miss Piggy."

"Stop calling her that. You've been out for revenge ever since I broke things off with you. I never thought you would stoop so low as to have me fired."

She walks away. "Nice knowing ya. It was fun while it lasted."

My chest pounds. I check the time. 10.12am. Will she still be on board? I can't remember what time her flight back to England is. I'm sure she told me at some point.

I stuff the tips and envelopes in my case and go to her cabin. The cleaners are already there, and it's empty. Fuck. I grab the handle of my suitcase and dash towards the exit. A row of yellow taxicabs line up along the dock and I jump in the first one. "Airport, please."

The drive seems to take forever. My heart hammers against my ribs like a shark thrashing in a cage. I call her phone, but it goes to voicemail. Please be there, please, please please.

I throw the driver a twenty—one of my tips. "Keep the change." Grabbing my case, I run towards the terminal and scan the boards for a flight to England. When I see it's not leaving until this afternoon, I relax a little knowing she hasn't left yet.

Searching the check-in area, her fake Louis Vuitton

luggage is stacked next to a pair of old vans and cropped leggings fitted snugly around those thick thighs. A check shirt drapes over her ass and her curls are tied up in a messy bun.

I've never seen her look this casual. So this is the real her when she's not putting on a show or trying to be someone she's not.

With tentative steps, I move closer. "Kitten."

She pivots, squeaking her vans against the tiled floor. "Zac. What are you doing here?"

"I had to see you before you left."

She folds her arms over her chest and bites the inside of her cheek. "What about your blonde dancer?"

"I don't know what you saw, but I was wasted that night. I don't even remember her kissing me. I must have erased that memory completely."

"Not on my account, I hope."

"Lizzie, look at me." I lift her chin and gaze into her teary crystal eyes. "I know you're not the one that got me fired. I'm sorry."

"You thought it was me?" Her forehead wrinkles and I swipe my thumb over them, hoping to erase all her worries.

"Yeah. I know now it was Jessica. Forgive me. For everything. Please." My fingers graze the softness of her cheek, and brush away a loose strand of hair, tucking it behind her ear.

"I'm sorry I called your mum those names. If I knew that was your mum in that photo, I wouldn't have—"

"Shh. I know, Lizzie." I bend my knees slightly and

crook my head to meet her mouth. I've missed these warm, plump, soft lips. My hands cup her face, and I tilt her head, taking full possession of her. I dip my tongue between her parted lips, hoping she will melt into me as she did before.

Her warm hands wrap around my neck and her body presses against my chest. She hums into my mouth, sending a vibration straight to my cock.

I hold her tight, not wanting to let her go. "Don't get on that plane. Stay with me."

She pulls her head back to look into my eyes. "I have to. I don't have anywhere to stay here. No job or anything."

"You don't have any of that in England do you? You can stay with me."

"But you don't have anywhere to stay either." She giggles.

"We can get a place together with the money we won. Please Lizzie. If you get on that plane, I worry I'll never see you again. We can check into a hotel tonight until we find somewhere more permanent. Or let me come to England with you. I don't care as long as we stay together."

"All right. I'll stay"

It takes a moment for what she said to register. My head shakes. I wasn't expecting her to agree so quickly. "You will? You're staying?"

She nods her head and a huge smile spreads across her beautiful face. Her blue eyes glisten like a pool in the summer sun. With a rush of adrenaline, I pick her up and spin her around in my arms.

She giggles again. "As long as you find a hotel with a laundrette because I don't have any clean underwear left."

"You won't be needing underwear when I get you in a room." I place her back down and her vans squeak on the polished floor.

She swats my chest then wraps her arms around me.

"I wasn't expecting you to say yes. I had a whole grovelling speech planned. I hadn't even got to the sucking ass part yet."

"You can get to that part in the hotel room."

I kiss her again, feeling like the luckiest man alive.

She pulls away, breaking the kiss. "And I'm going to need to hear that grovelling speech at some point."

"Anything else you want, kitten?"

She chews on the inside of her mouth. "No more flirting with other women."

"I can't promise that."

She sighs and looks down.

I lift her chin. "I don't know I'm flirting half the time. Be patient with me? I can promise you're the only woman in the world for me, and I want to spend the rest of my life showing you that. Meet me half way and trust me."

"I do trust you, Zac."

I throw one of her bags over my shoulder and pull my suitcase while holding her hand. We walk out of the airport together, ready to start our next adventure.

CHAPTER
Twenty one

LIZZIE

Three Months Later

"Good to see you, sis." My brother Ed meets me at the airport, wrapping me up in a big bear hug.

I give him a squeeze. "How's Susie and my favourite niece?"

"Everyone is good. Come on, let's get you home." He takes my suitcase from me. "Didn't you have like three of these when you went?"

"I thought I would leave them in LA. As soon as my temporary working visa comes through, I'm going back. I couldn't see the point in bringing everything back with me."

"How long for the visa? It's ridiculously long-winded. Although, I'm glad you had to come home. We missed you."

"I missed you too."

Stepping out of the terminal, the summer sun heats my face. It's really warm and muggy for the end of May in England.

Eddie lifts my case into the boot of his car. "So what's happening with you and this Zachariah?"

I tilt my head and frown at him. "His name is Zachary, and you will like him."

Ed jumps in the driver's side. "Am I ever going to meet him?"

Sliding into the passenger seat, I pull on my seatbelt. "I'll invite you to the wedding." I giggle.

Eddie's face drops. "Has he proposed?"

"No. I'm just messing with you."

He starts the engine. "Is it serious, then? I'm guessing it is seeing as you stayed over there with him for the last three months."

"I think so. We just bought a place, and he put my name on the deeds."

"Susie told me about that old building you bought. She showed me the photos you sent her. Are you sure you know what you're doing? It seems like a waste of money to me."

"It has so much potential. Zac knows what he's doing. Besides, it's his dream and his money."

"What about your dream?"

"What about it?"

"You always wanted to run your own little coffee shop."

"Well, now I'll help Zac run an Italian cafe. We hope to turn it into a restaurant one day."

I pull my phone out and text him.

'Just landed. I'm in the car with my brother now. How's things?'

A few minutes later, he replies.

'How was the flight? All good here. I've just woke up. Missing you already.'

My heart aches for him. We haven't spent a night apart since we left the ship. I wish I was there now, waking up next to him. I hold the phone close to my chest and think about how we would spend our mornings. He would always bring me a coffee in bed, still waiting on me hand and foot. One of the things I love about him. The smile on my face makes my jaw ache. I do love him, but I haven't even told him that yet. I was waiting for him to say it first.

I text back. 'Wish I was there with you. I'll call you later.'

Ed taps his fingers on the steering wheel. "What's lover boy up to then?"

"Hmm?" I turn to Ed.

He nods at my phone. "That was him, wasn't it? You were grinning like the Cheshire Cat high on crack."

"He was just saying he missed me. He's just woken up. It's only morning over there."

Ed nods. "Do you have jet lag?"

"I am tired. I might just have a nap while you drive home."

"Go for it. You won't get much nap time at home. Rosie is dying to see you."

"And I her." My only regret living in LA is not seeing my niece, Rosie, grow up. Plus, I miss my brother and his wife, Susie. She's like a sister to me.

But I do love it in LA; being near the ocean, the vibrancy and glamour of it all. Though our apartment was anything but glamorous with no air con, but I would sleep anywhere if it meant being with Zac.

We wanted to save as much of our money as possible to use as a deposit for our business. He secured himself a job serving at a high-end restaurant and in the day he's been renovating our new place. I never knew he was so handy at DIY.

I spent my days there too. I'm quite handy with a paintbrush, and I can't work until my visa comes through, so I kept myself busy. Although most of the time I was ogling Zac shirtless.

I close my eyes, sad I won't be there for the grand opening next month.

ZAC

AFTER TEXTING HER BACK, I drag myself out of bed. I meant what I said. I'm missing her already, her vanilla and honey scent, her warm snuggly body, and her cuddles at night.

While making coffee, I see the mug I bought her with a cute kitten on with the words, 'You're purr-fect.' Using her cup, hoping to feel a little closer to her this morning, I pour myself a drink.

Once dressed, I head to our cafe. I have the builders in today fitting the counter and the kitchen area. Lizzie did a fantastic job at painting. She painted everything from top to bottom. The upstairs bathroom just needs fitting, then it is habitable.

By the time she comes home, I want it all done so she can move straight in. I wanted our first night here to be the both of us, so we camped out last week and slept in the master bedroom, bringing over a few blankets—not that we got much sleep.

The meeting with a sign company comes around quickly, after a busy morning with renovations. I tell them the name of the cafe and we discuss a logo, lighting and materials.

After the meeting, it's time for my shift at Alessandro's. The owner was a family friend of my nonno's and said there will always be a job for me there, but I'm handing in my notice tonight. I need to be all hands on deck when our cafe opens.

Josh has also handed his notice in on the ship, and next month, when his contract ends, he will come to work for me. He's the closest thing I have to a brother. We went to school together, and the only person I would trust with my business other than Lizzie.

At work, Sara walks over to the bar with another drinks order in her hand. "Table six wants one of your special cocktails for Margery's birthday, a bottle of Vino Rosso, and two pints of Stella." She hands me the order. "And table three are on a girls' night out. They asked for the hot waiter that makes cocktails."

My eyes narrow. "What did you say?"

"I told them you'd be over shortly. Have to keep the customers happy."

"Send Alfie."

She frowns. Alfie is many things, but hot isn't one of them. Sara spins on her heel, leaving me to get the drinks.

I finish Margery's special birthday cocktail and deliver it to her myself. A lovely woman who was a good friend of the family.

"Happy birthday to you." I sing the words and light the sparkler in the red drink.

"Thank you, my dear." She squeezes my cheeks together like she used to when I was five. "Such a nice boy. Your ma would be so proud of you, Zac."

"Happy birthday, Margery." I kiss her cheek. "Enjoy."

I walk over to table three with the cackle of girls. "What can I get you ladies to drink?"

A brunette says, "She'll have whatever that is if it comes with a kiss. It's her birthday too." She points to a young blonde in front of me who blushes and looks down at the table.

I smile. "One birthday cocktail coming right up, although I'll pass on the kissing. My girlfriend won't be too happy about me kissing another girl. Margery over there doesn't count, she's practically my aunt."

The girl glares at her friend, looking a little deflated. That's not how I want her to feel on her birthday.

"How about a cocktail on the house? Seeing as it's your birthday."

Her face lights up and she nods. "Thank you, that's very kind of you. Your girlfriend is a lucky girl."

"If you met her, you'd see I'm the lucky one."

The girls all awe in unison, and I continue with their order.

When I have quick break, I check my phone to see a missed call. We haven't thought this through with the time difference. I call her back.

"Lizzie."

"Hello, it's good to hear your voice. I forgot you'd be at

work now. I'm just about to sleep and wanted to say goodnight." She sounds tired.

"Have you had a good day?" I rub the ache in my chest, knowing I'll be going home to a lonely apartment tonight.

"It's been nice seeing everyone, but I'm exhausted."

"I bet."

"My brother wants to meet you." A smile is behind her voice.

"Should I be worried?" I've seen her brother when she's been on FaceTime. He's a big guy, and quite protective of his little sister, though he has nothing to worry about with me. Nobody could love her more.

"No, he's a big softie, really."

"Like you, then." I chuckle.

"You should be thankful, or I wouldn't have put up with you for the last three months."

"Is that what you've been doing? I thought it was me putting up with you." I'd put up with her any day of the week, even when she's moaning at me for leaving a towel on the bed, or dirty pots on the counter.

"You weren't saying that the other night when you were begging me to stay. Illegally, I might add."

"I'm a glutton for punishment. What can I say?" I would have locked her away if I could. She would never have left.

She giggles down the line.

"Lizzie, I have to get back to work."

"I'll call you tomorrow then, or you call me."

"Sure." I want to tell her I love her. Fuck, why haven't I

done that already? I've loved her from the first day I laid eyes on her. I just didn't know it then.

"Night, night."

"Goodnight, kitten." I can't tell her I love her for the first time over the phone. That needs to be special. I should have done it before she left. I'm such a chicken-shit.

I check my emails while on my break and receive a link to the website for the cafe. It looks great. The menu needs tweaking. I'm not sure I can offer all this that we had planned with just me at the moment, but I love the logo and the design of the site. Lizzie will love it. I'm not going to tell her, though. It will be a surprise for her when she comes back home.

CHAPTER
Twenty two

LIZZIE

Two Months Later

I LEAN over the counter next to the cash register at the pet shop where I work now. This isn't how I saw my career panning out, but it's a job to tide me over until I can move back to the States. At least I can pay my brother back while I'm here. He refuses to take rent, but I buy food and stuff for them. He never refuses food.

"Are you dreaming about your Italian?" Emma says as she opens a box of dog chews ready to go on the shelf.

"He's American, but yes."

"I can't believe your visa hasn't come through yet. How long has it been?"

My chin rests in the palm of my hand while I tap my nails on the counter with my other hand. "It's been five months since I applied. Two months since I've seen Zac."

"Awe, that's so hard. I don't understand why it takes so long."

"Me neither. I just want to be with him, you know?"

She rubs my back. "Girl, if I had an Italian fella like Zac, I'd want to be with him too. I hear ya."

"He's American." I shake my head and smile.

"Here, put these on the shelf. Give you something to take your mind off him."

I take a handful of squeaky dog toys to the middle aisle and neatly position them on the shelf.

"How long have you worked here?" A gruff voice says behind me.

I turn to see Dwayne with a large bag of dog food in his hand resting on his hip. He never wanted a dog before.

I furrow my brow. "What's it to you?"

His girlfriend waddles up behind him with an enormous belly. My mouth gapes. She must be ready to drop, confirming they were at it for months behind my back—as I suspected.

She blanks me and hooks her arm through Dwayne's, pulling him to the counter. I'm so glad I don't have to serve them. My stomach aches as all the feelings of worthlessness come flooding back to me.

I miss Zac more than ever. The feel of his arms wrapped around me and the scruff of his jaw rubbing against my skin. The way he would kiss me mid conversation because he couldn't resist having me for one more second. I can't even call him. He'll still be asleep now. The time difference is so annoying.

I glance over to the counter to see her eyes boring into me like I'm the one that hurt her. She rubs her palm over her baby bump and smirks.

With a sigh, I look away. She's welcome to that piece of shit. Zac's triple the man Dwayne is. He picks the food up from the counter and glances at me before walking out of the shop. I walk back to the till to collect more chew toys from Emma with a trembling hand.

"Are you okay?"

I nod. "She's welcome to him."

After work, I have a missed call from Zac. I sit in my car parked outside the store so I can still use the wi-fi and FaceTime him.

"Morning, kitten." His hair is all messy and his eyes look tired, like he hasn't been awake long.

"It's afternoon here. I've done a full day's work already." I smile at the screen, gazing into his sleepy eyes.

"How was your day?"

"It was okay." I don't want to talk about Dwayne on the phone to Zac. "I miss you."

"Believe me, Lizzie, I miss you. I miss you so fucking much." He holds the phone down so I can see his morning wood. "Look, he misses you too." He pulls his shorts away from his waist so I can get a good look.

I giggle. "Okay, stop winking at me. Let me see your gorgeous face."

He pulls the camera back to him and runs his hand through his messy hair. I want to say I love you, but all we ever say is I miss you. It's like neither one of us wants to be the one to say it first.

But I'm going to say it. I can't wait any longer, needing to hear the words back, and I want him to know I really do love him.

"I love you, Zac." My throat closes up as I say his name and I hold my breath, waiting for him to say it too.

He stares at me through the screen. "Kitten." His head leans back against the headboard, and he closes his eyes. The screen goes to the swallow on his chest, then it goes dark.

"Are you still there?"

"I'm here."

There's another long pause. I try to swallow the lump in my throat, but it won't go down.

"Kitten, I have to go. I'll call you later."

"Okay." I cancel the call. The lump in my throat grows and the tears build in the corner of my eyes. I blink, letting them fall down my cheek. Why didn't he say it back? I was sure he loved me and was just being a dick, not wanting to say it first.

Driving home, I can't help but wonder what's going on with Zac. Does he not feel the same? Is that why he doesn't want to tell me he loves me? Is he going to let me down? A million scenarios go through my mind as emptiness creeps into my heart. His calls are less frequent lately. I thought it was because he was busy with the cafe, but is he just losing interest? I'm not exactly a barrel of laughs when he calls. All I do is work and go home to my brother's. The highlight of my day is playing with my niece.

I trudge into the house and slump on the sofa.

"What's up with you?" My brother says.

"What?"

"You have a face like a smacked arse."

"Thanks. Anything else you want to say? Kick me while I'm down."

"What's happened?"

"Did you know Dwayne was having a kid?"

"You're not still letting him get to you, are you? I thought you'd moved on."

"I have. I was just shocked to see him and *her* with a massive belly, that's all."

I sit in the chair and sigh, picking at the hem of my work t-shirt. "I told Zac I loved him today, but he never said it back."

"So that's what's wrong. Do you think you're flogging a dead horse?"

"I love him though."

"But if he doesn't love you by now. What's the point in moving over there to get your heart broken again?"

"I know you're right." A tear escapes me and I sniffle.

Rosie toddles over, holding a game. "Auntie Lizzie, will you play with me?"

"Sure." I glance at the board game, snakes and ladders. I can do that.

After dinner, we all watch the new Toy Story movie. By the end of the film, I'm in floods of tears. Ed carries a sleeping Rosie to bed.

Susie hands me a tissue. "You've been over emotional lately. Are you sure you're not pregnant?"

I dry my eyes. "It was a sad film. Those heart warming movies always get to me, you know what I'm like."

She pulls out her phone, opening the calendar app. "When was your last period?"

My brother enters the room, clearing his throat with bulging eyes. "You're not up the duff, are you?"

I let out a long sigh. "No. I'm not pregnant."

"If he's left you knocked up, I'll fly over there and kick his arse."

Susie gives my brother a stern look and a nod for him

to leave us alone. He rolls his eyes and heads into the kitchen.

Susie goes back to her calendar app. "Can you remember your last period?"

"I haven't had a period since I changed my pill in LA to the shot."

"I see. You had that tummy bug a few weeks ago when you threw up. Are you still feeling sick?"

I shake my head, dismissing her. I only feel sick occasionally. It's like I never fully recovered from the sickness bug. "I'll be fine I'm definitely not pregnant and I'm just tired and missing Zac." I think.

"Try taking some evening primrose. It could just be hormones." She squeezes my hand and gives me a sympathetic smile.

"Thanks. I'm sure it's just because I miss Zac." I check my phone again, waiting for him to call me like he said he would. It will be the afternoon now in LA.

I take myself to bed and call him instead, but it goes straight to voicemail. He either has no signal, or he's on another call.

Fifteen minutes later, I try him again, but nothing.

I text, 'Please call me. It doesn't matter if you wake me, I just need to hear your voice.'

Struggling to keep my eyes open, I try Zac one more time, getting his voicemail again.

Heavy breaths leave my lungs as I jump up in a cold, sticky sweat. I was in hospital, giving birth. Alone. A lump fills my throat as I gasp for air. Was it a premonition?

I check my phone. It's 4.28am, and he still hasn't called. I scroll his social media for any clue of what he's up to. It still says he's single, but that's nothing new. He's never changed it to be in a relationship with me. Another tear falls, and I wipe it away with my hand.

I don't want to be one of those girlfriends that needs to know every little detail of their boyfriend's life. He's not Dwayne and I have no reason not to trust him. I just want to know he loves me.

Calling him again, I get his voicemail. "Zac, please call me. I'm getting worried about you."

I place the phone next to my pillow and hold it in my hand so I can feel it vibrate when he calls.

"Auntie Lizzie, wake up, wake up. Come and get your birthday present." Rosie jumps up and down on my bed. I blink open my eyes to Susie opening the curtains.

"Are you all right Lizzie? It's almost 10am."

"I didn't sleep well last night." I wipe the drool from my chin and sit up.

"Were you excited about your birthday?" Rosie says.

I smile. "Yes, that's it."

"Come down, Rosie. Let auntie Lizzie get up and get ready. She can open your present when she comes downstairs."

They both walk out of the room. I check my phone and still nothing. I call him again. "Zac. Please call me."

I clean my teeth and tie my hair up in a messy bun, leaving my pyjamas on. It is a Sunday after all and my birthday, so I figure I can have a pyjama day if I want.

Walking into the kitchen, my brother pours me a coffee. "I can't stomach that, Ed." The smell makes me gag. I'm sure it's just because I'm worried sick about Zac.

I lean against the worktop. "Has Zac called the house at all this morning?"

"No. Has he still not called you back?"

I shake my head. "Do you think I scared him off by telling him I loved him?"

Ed sips on the drink he made for me. "Put it this way, if you did, he ain't the one, sis."

"I thought he would have at least called me on my birthday."

Susie tidies some breakfast cereal away. "Your birthday isn't over yet. Perhaps he's asleep and will call you later."

"Don't stick up for him, Sue. He needs his arse kicking."

She rolls her eyes. "Can you call the cafe when it opens?"

I grab the milk and pour some into a glass. "If he hasn't called me by then I will, yes."

"Anyway, happy birthday." Ed hands me a small box wrapped in silver paper. I open it up and see a pair of earrings with blue topaz jewels hanging in a tear droplet.

"These are stunning."

"I thought they matched Mum's necklace that you always wear."

I throw my arms around my brother and give him a tight squeeze. "I love them."

He lifts his drink and nods towards me. "They match your eyes."

"Thank you so much." I hold them up to the window and watch them sparkle in the morning sun.

Rosie comes up to me with a larger gift, wrapped in

pink wrapping paper that is folded all messy. "Open my present now."

I take it from her and rip it open. "Thank you so much, Rosie. A Gryffindor hoodie. I love it."

"Now we can match."

"That will be cool." I give her a big hug then pull on the sweater over my pyjamas.

A phone buzzes. My heart stops as I scramble to it on the counter. My shoulders slump when I see a text from Emma at work, wishing me a happy birthday. I text back and then hit Zac's number again. It goes to the answering machine.

I walk into the hallway to leave a message. "Zac, please call me. I'm sorry, I never meant to say I love you. If I scared you off, I'm sorry. Just call me so I know you're okay. I'm really worried about you."

I lean against the wall in the hallway. I don't want anyone to see my tears. The usual busy sounds filter in from outside. A car engine comes to a halt and a door slams. My phone buzzes. I look at the screen to see Zac's number flash up and my heart hurtles to life as if zapped with a defibrillator.

"Where have you been? I've been worried sick." I snap. Not sure whether I should be happy or angry.

"My phone died. I've just had it charging in the cab."

"What cab?"

"What's this about you not meaning to say I love you?"

"What?"

"Are you saying you don't love me?"

"Well, do you even love me?"

The doorbell rings. I'm right next to the front door, so I open it with a huff.

My mouth drops. The phone slips from my ear, and I shove it in my hoodie pocket.

"You're really here." My heart is doing a hundred beats per minute.

Zac pops his phone back in his jeans pocket. With both hands, he takes hold of my face. "I'll show you how much I love you." He tilts my head and takes possession of my mouth. His tongue dips and swirls around mine, making me dizzy.

The hallway spins into a blur. The only thing I see is Zac. He's all I feel and hear. Breaking the kiss, his lips trail along my jaw, down my neck, kisses of devotion adorning my skin. He comes back to my lips. "I love you so much, kitten. So fucking much. I had to tell you in person."

Tears roll down my face, but this time they're happy tears. "I love you, Zac." I throw my arms around him, and he kisses my neck again.

"I need to be inside you. Now." He pushes me against the wall. His fingers tug at the hem of my hoodie, trying to find his way underneath. He pulls back to look at it, pulling his eyebrows together. "I thought you were a Hufflepuff?"

"Shh." I spot Rosie in the corner of my eye and clear my throat. "Zac."

He continues to kiss my neck and tug at the jumper.

"Zac, this is my niece."

His eyes widen, and he turns around. My brother walks into the hall with a coffee in his hand, followed by Susie.

"Eddie, this is Zac. Zac, my brother and his wife, Susie."

He shakes Ed's hand and gives Susie a hug, then bends down to Rosie. "I've heard all about you. Someone told me you like sweets."

She nods. Zac pulls his suitcase in from the front step and unzips the front pocket, pulling out a big bag of Haribo's and hands them to her.

"Thank you." She runs off with them in her hand.

"Where's my gift? It's my birthday."

He smiles. "I ate your Haribo's in the taxicab, but I saved this for you." He pulls out a small box from his pocket, then gets down on one knee.

I gasp, covering my mouth with my hands. "Zac."

"Lizzie, I'm taking you back to the States as my wife. I love you more than life itself. Marry me." It was more of a command than a request. A party popper of glitter and rainbows bursts in my chest. With watery eyes, I glance at my brother, but can still make out his face, gawking at the two of us, and Susie, who is tearing up as much as me.

Zac opens the box. A beautiful solitaire diamond stares back at me, glistening just like my eyes.

"Of course I'll marry you. I love you, Zac."

He stands, wraps his arms around me, and kisses me again.

"Happy birthday, kitten."

EPILOGUE

LIZZIE
Four Weeks Later

ZAC HAILS a cab as we exit the airport. My ring catches my eye, sparkling in the LA sun. A whimsical smile lifts my cheeks as I admire the platinum band nestled next to the modest diamond.

After lifting our luggage into the boot of a taxi, we slip into the back seat. With my temporary working visa now approved, I'm allowed back in the States. Zac has applied for a temporary green card for marriage and then in two years I can apply for the permit.

I rest my head on Zac's shoulder in the taxi and yawn as he interlaces his fingers with mine and gives my hand a gentle squeeze.

"The flight's taken it out of you, huh?"

I yawn again as he says the words, nodding, then I let out a blissful hum. Closing my eyes, I think of our wedding two weeks ago.

A small affair. Eddie walked me down the aisle in my blush lace gown that I bought off the peg in the sale, and Rosie was thrilled to be our flower girl. It was all a bit rushed but the vicar slotted us in at our local village church where my parents were married. My aunt—Mum's sister—made it at short notice and our cousins, as well as a few of my friends.

We had a meal afterwards at a local hotel, but not before Zac snuck us away to our room; a wedding gift from Ed and Susie. Eddie said there was no way we were going back to his place on our wedding night.

Zac nudges me awake. "We're home, kitten."

I gaze out of the window at our cafe ahead. It was a shell when I left and has clearly had a facelift. "Are we here already?"

As the taxi comes to a halt, the Italian mural frosted window design is the first thing I see. Stepping out of the car, the signage comes into view. My mouth drops open and a lump forms in my throat, making me speechless. "When...how did...?"

Zac grins. "I had it done before I came to England."

He lifts my case out of the boot along with his own, and the driver drives off.

I throw my arms around him. "What happened to Marco's?"

"This dream was only possible because of you. Since I signed the deed, it was always going to be called *Lizzie's*."

A tear escapes me, and Zac kisses it away. "Come on, let me show you the renovations."

The door dings as Zac pulls both suitcases into the cafe, and Josh looks up from behind the counter. He bounds over and gives Zac a few jabs to the ribs before wrapping me up in his arms and lifting me onto my tiptoes.

"Not too tight. Be careful with her," Zac says. He's been so overprotective these last few weeks.

"Right, sorry." Josh gently releases me and my small

heels clink on the laminate floor. "I'll take your cases up. I've been crashing in the spare room, looking after the place while you've been gone." Josh turns to a young girl waitressing. "Millie, hold the fort while I help Zac with the cases."

"Hey Millie, this is my wife, Lizzie," Zac says before lugging the cases through to the back.

She forms an O with her mouth and looks like she's about to curtsy. "You're *the* Lizzie?"

I look around to check she's talking to me and not Liz Hurley or some other famous Hollywood actress. Although the way she's looking at me, you'd think I was the queen of England. "Hello, I guess I am." I extend my hand and greet her.

"Ma'am, please take a seat. Let me get some refreshments after your journey. I'll get you a pot of English tea." She pulls a leather tub chair out from a round table and fluffs a cushion, gesturing for me to sit.

I gratefully sink into the seat. "Thank you. Millie, is it?"

"Yes ma'am. Can I get you anything else, ma'am?" She bends her knees and there it is; the curtsy she's been holding back since I walked in.

"You can call me Lizzie." I give her my biggest smile and shrug my jacket off as a hot flush comes over me, along with a sudden bout of nausea.

She smiles and scurries off behind the counter, leaving me to take in my surroundings. The hanging vines from the beams on the ceiling intertwined with hanging lights give off a Mediterranean vibe, and the black and white pictures of his grandparents and his mother hanging on the wall are a lovely touch for a small family business.

Zac returns and takes a seat. "Everything all right?"

"I'm just feeling a little sick. It's the smell of the coffee. I'll be all right. It's not as bad as it has been recently."

"Millie, do we have any ginger cookies?" He says, taking my hand with concern in his eyes.

Ever since we found out I was pregnant on our honeymoon, he's been more attentive than before. There's no wonder Millie is treating me like royalty because that's exactly how Zac makes me feel; like his queen. And I use the term honeymoon loosely. It was a weekend away in a friend's caravan at the seaside, but it gave us time to share the old haunts I explored as a kid when my family went on caravan holidays on the East Coast.

After retching at the smell of his morning coffee—something I used to love—he knew something was off with me. My stomach was in knots, waiting for the line to appear on the test—or not appear. I wasn't sure how I'd feel and I wasn't sure how Zac would feel, even though he reassured me he is nothing like his father and I'm stuck with him, whatever the outcome. I'm sure I saw a hint of a tear in his eyes when the two lines appeared. Then he took my face in his rough hands and peppered me with kisses.

Millie places a tray on the table—a pot of tea and a plate of biscuits—disturbing my trip down memory lane. "Can I get you anything, Mr Walters?"

"I'll have some of this tea. Thanks, Millie, and how many times do I have to tell you to call me Zac?"

"Sorry, sir." She smiles and slips away.

Josh takes a seat with us, holding up a menu he and Zac designed. "What do you think, Lizzie?"

"Everything looks amazing." I look at Zac. "No

wonder you were exhausted every time I called." All of it was done on a tight budget too, and he even saved a few quid so we could get married. Nothing fancy, but our wedding couldn't have been more perfect.

Zac smiles and pours my tea. "I've been dying to show you the website and the menus and stuff, but I wanted the name to be a surprise."

"I love it."

Zac reaches over the small wooden table for two and kisses my lips.

"All right, you two. There's a room upstairs for that." Josh chuckles and Zac breaks our kiss.

"Thanks for keeping this place running, bro."

"Don't worry about it."

"I'm serious. I don't know what I would've done without you taking care of business while I was in England."

"Does that mean I'm getting a raise?"

"You'll get a pay raise when I get one. We want to make you a partner."

Josh straightens his shoulders. "Are you serious?"

"Yeah, Lizzie's gonna be out of action for a while and I need my right hand man. I've already had the documents arranged. You just need to sign. Don't get too excited. The bank still owns most of this place, but with Lizzie's ideas and our experience in hospitality, I reckon we can make a success and pay off the loan. Gradually build it up. What do you think? Then we can make more renovations."

"Sounds great."

Millie brings Josh a cold drink and smiles at him as she slides it along the table.

"Hey Millie, you're now looking at a partner."

She looks between him and Zac. "For real?"

Josh stands and picks her up. She squeals with excitement and kicks her legs as Josh squeezes her bottom.

I glance at Zac, who looks puzzled.

Zac waves his hand between the two of them. "Are you two—"

Josh's lips press against Millie's, and he just answered Zac's question without saying a word.

Josh breaks the kiss, pats Millie on the bottom, and with blushed cheeks, she rushes back to the counter.

Zac leans back in the chair with a smirk playing in the corner of his mouth. "So, when did that happen?"

"We're just friends." A family walks through the doors. "I'll catch up with you later. Some of us actually work around here." He smiles and walks away to greet the customers.

I finish my tea and yawn.

Zac stands and takes my hand. "Let me take you to bed."

"Hmm, I like the sound of that." It will be nice to get into bed in a place of our own. As much as I loved living with my brother and his family, there wasn't much privacy.

Zac pulls me from the chair and leads me to the back, past the kitchen and up the stairs. The keys jangle from his pocket as we approach our apartment door. When we bought this place, the wallpaper was hanging from the wall where a leak in the roof had caused damp to seep through. There were no carpets on the floor and the rooms smelt fusty.

He turns the key, and holding the handle, opens the door an inch. "It's not finished."

I cover his hand with mine. "We can finish it together." I push the door open a little wider, desperate to see what he's done with the place.

Zac pulls me back. "Wait up. I almost forgot." He scoops me up by the legs and lifts me bridal style. "I always wanted to do that, like in the movies."

He carries me over the threshold and kicks the door shut behind us.

"You can put me down now. I know I'm heavy."

"I'm never putting you down, kitten." He carries me through the warm grey living room. I lift my feet so I don't catch the new grey sofa and my eyes are drawn to the large TV hanging on the wall.

Entering the bedroom, the last time I was in here there was nothing but a mattress on the floor and a few blankets and pillows when we spent the night here before I moved back to England. Now it's beautiful. Zac has hung the wallpaper I picked out on one wall, matching the blush colour I painted in here.

He lays me down on the large bed, tossing the throw and scatter cushions to the floor, and hovers over me, caging me between his biceps.

My fingers sweep the curl from his forehead, then move to the scar on his temple. "We made it, Zac. It wasn't always plain sailing, but we made it."

"When I saw you on that first day, I knew I was in deep water." With his tender lips, he peppers my face with kisses before swooping in to crush my mouth.

My stomach flutters like birds on the ocean breeze, and I deepen our kiss.

"You wanna christen this new bed now or later?" His erection digs into my hip as he grinds his pelvis against me and wiggles his eyebrows.

I giggle. "Now, please."

His hands slide up my dress and find the elastic to my knickers. I lift my bottom to free them as he tugs them down. They dangle from my ankles while he undoes the strap of my sandal.

My body vibrates with excitement, as it always does when he has me like this.

"Start unbuttoning that dress, kitten. I have zero patience and when I've taken these sandals off, that dress is the next thing to go."

My fingers fumble with the buttons on my shirt dress. Once my sandals are off, my knickers drop to the floor. Zac plants soft kisses along my leg, up my thigh and over my sensitive area that I keep trimmed in a heart just for him. He kneels on the bed, whips off his t-shirt and unbuttons his jeans. My breathing accelerates, seeing his throbbing length as he releases it from his boxer shorts.

"Take that bra off, too. I want you fully naked." He pulls off his jeans and the last of his garments while I sit up and pull my arms from the dress and bra straps. He tosses the clothes on the floor and cages me beneath him. My legs open and his erection rubs against my slickness. His mouth sucks on my neck, and I pant his name.

He slips into my wet heat, and I wrap my legs around him, needing more of him inside me.

ANNIE CHARME

Keeping control, he gently rocks at a steady pace, not his usual plundering that has me screaming with pleasure.

"Zac, what's wrong? Stop teasing me, please."

He stops all movement, although he can't stop his trembling as he hovers above me. "I don't wanna hurt the baby."

My heart swells as a wave of love comes crashing down on me. "You won't hurt the baby. He's perfectly safe."

His eyebrows pinch. "He? You know something I don't?"

I shake my head. "I just have a feeling, that's all."

"When do we find out?"

"At the next scan. If it's a boy, I'd like to call him Marco, after your middle name and your nonno. You may not have called the cafe Marco's as planned, but I want our son to be called it. And if it's a girl we'll call her Lillian after your ma."

"No we won't."

I squish my eyebrows together and he kisses the wrinkle away.

"We'll call her Lillian-Rose, after both our mothers."

"My ship really did come in when I met you."

He pushes in further, but slow and gentle, until settled deep inside, filling me with love. We fit perfectly together as our body's move in sync at a steady rhythm. With his eyes locked on mine, I breathe him in. The pressure builds in my centre. I can't stop the tingles that travel through every limb of my body, making my toes curl and my back arch. My sex pulses around him, and he groans out his own release.

212

When we come together, it's like two shooting stars colliding, and for a moment, we are the brightest light in the heavens.

ZAC

Valentine's Day, The Following Year.

A LOOSE CURL falls over her face and I brush it back behind her ear, grazing her soft cheek with my fingertips. Her round belly presses against mine as she moves closer, cuddling up to my chest with a soft hum from her lips.

"Morning, kitten."

She squeezes me tight. "I don't want to get up yet."

"You don't have to move." I kiss her forehead. I don't want to get up either, but I have a lot to do today. We have a full house booked for Valentine's. "You can stay in bed. I'll sort everything."

"Just stay in bed with me for five more minutes."

I can't say no to that. A grin spreads across my face. "Oh yeah? What do you have in mind?" She looks up at my face, opening her eyes, and I raise an eyebrow.

She giggles. "Don't get any ideas."

"What? The midwife said it was good to help dilate everything down there. I'm only trying to help things along."

"Ugh. Any excuse to get me to bend over."

I chuckle. She's right though. I'll take any opportunity I can.

"Happy Valentine's, Lizzie."

Her eyes open fully, and a smile pushes her cheeks up. "I forgot it's Valentine's." She pecks my lips, then shuffles to the edge of the bed, opens her nightstand drawer, and pulls out a small bag. "I know we said no gifts because we're saving for the baby, but I saw this and wanted to get you a little something."

I take the bag from her and take out a silver keyring with words inscribed, 'I Love You, Daddy'. A warmth spreads across my chest. "I always wanted you to call me *Daddy*."

She swats my arm and giggles again. "You're going to be an amazing daddy."

"I already am. Now be a good girl and bend over." I squeeze her meaty thighs in an attempt to roll her onto her side.

"Zac, stop fooling around."

"Kiss me then, at least."

She straddles me, takes my face between her palms and presses her lips to mine. I can't believe it's been a full year since we met on the ship. A year to the day since we made love on Valentine's night. Time flies when you're having fun, and this last year with her has been one of the best years of my life.

My hands ride up under her pyjama top that says, 'Baby On Board'. Her tits are bigger than ever and her nipples are more prominent and sensitive. A moan escapes her lips as my thumb moves over the pebbled nubs and her hips rock gently over my throbbing dick.

I knew all it would take is a kiss from my lips, a stroke

of my thumb. She can't resist me. Especially when I'm naked under her or over her.

"Zac," she whispers, gazing into my eyes.

I pat her bottom. "All right. I have to get up now. Things to do."

She narrows her eyes, and squeezes her thighs, preventing me from moving. "You're not going anywhere."

I quirk a grin. "On your knees then, kitten. I have about ten minutes before the deliveries arrive."

She scrambles to her knees and positions herself on all fours. Her round ass in my face covered in her pink pyjama shorts, like a ripe peach waiting for me to take a bite. I pull the fabric down, letting them drop to her knees as she kneels on the bed. My hand strokes between her damp thighs and I sink my fingers into her wet heat to check she's ready for me.

Positioning myself behind her, I slowly enter her, filling up her channel until she envelopes me like being wrapped up tight in a duvet. My eyes flicker as the pressure builds in the pit of my stomach and I dig my fingers into her fleshy hips as I pull out slowly and re-enter, making sure I stay in control. Her arms quiver and her body trembles like it always does when I'm inside her.

When I'm balls deep like this, there's no better feeling, though I miss seeing her face full of wonder while I make love to her. My tip presses against her cervix, reaching parts of her that can only be reached from this position, and a wave of goosebumps prickle my skin, making my heart rate speed up a notch, along with my movements, but I make sure I'm gentle.

My legs shake as I try to keep control, and her whimpers get louder. Her walls clamp down around me so I know she's coming, and I chase my own release, feeling the pulse from deep within her, joined by my throbbing dick as my balls tighten. I kiss her back, wrapping my arm under her belly to hold her steady while she rides out her orgasm.

I pull out and she collapses onto the bed. I move the hair from her face and kiss her lips. "Don't move. Back in a minute." Grabbing some jeans, I make my way downstairs, where I hid her gift.

When I return, she's sitting up in bed, stroking her stomach. "The baby's awake."

I hold up the bunch of flowers that I was hiding and watch her face brighten. A smile pushes her glowing cheeks up as she takes in the sight of the Hawaiian bouquet.

"Zac. They're beautiful."

I break off a pink tropical flower and place it behind her ear. "Not as beautiful as you." My lips press against hers and then against her belly, before pressing my ear there. The familiar sound of our child's heartbeat fills my ears, along with a growl from Lizzie's empty stomach, reminding me I should fix her some breakfast.

Her fingers stroke the hair from my forehead. "I thought we weren't getting gifts for Valentine's."

I smile up at her as she holds the flowers and inhales the sweet fragrance.

"It's not a Valentine's gift. It's our anniversary gift."

The doorbell rings through the apartment, making me jolt. "That'll be the delivery."

STANDING behind the bar in our thriving restaurant, I glance at the next order and pick up the cocktail shaker. Last month, we went from a coffee shop to a restaurant after hiring an amazing Italian chef, Luca. We now serve meals and alcohol, as well as the usual sweet treats and the best Italian coffee.

Shaking the metal cocktail maker, I focus on Lizzie taking orders, even though I told her to rest.

She laughs with the customers, scribbling on the notepad in her hand. An elderly woman pats Lizzie on her full, round belly. I never thought Lizzie could be more beautiful, but she's glowing, emitting a radiant aura around her and our child. My heart stutters as she pushes the hair from her face, her rounded belly brushing the back of the chairs as she squeezes through the gaps. She catches me looking and smiles, causing another stutter in my chest.

Josh approaches the bar. "Have you done those drinks yet?"

"What?" I pinch my eyebrows.

"Table 9. Drinks order. Capeesh?" Josh shakes his head with a grin.

"Right. Table 9 drinks order, coming up." I grab a pint and pull the lever on the pump.

Lizzie waddles over with another order in her hand and a smile on her face. "Table 6 wants a bottle of Pino and two bottles of Bud."

I kiss her forehead, placing my hands on her waist to

pull her close to me. Her belly rests against my stomach and my hands move over the bump. "How's our girl doing?"

"Lillian-Rose is kicking up a storm in here. I think she's on a sugar high from the cake I ate earlier."

"Put your feet up. Josh, Millie and I will manage tonight."

"Zac, I'm fine. I might be due any day, but I can still help take orders. Besides, I enjoy being down here with you when you're working."

"You like to keep an eye on me?" I smirk.

"Yes, but only because I fancy the pants off you." She pecks my lips. "Table 3 are on a hen night. Fix the bride-to-be one of your specialities on the house." She pecks my lips again before shuffling away to take more orders. I once said she was a shooting star, but she's so much more. My woman and our baby girl are my universe.

I finish the drinks for table 9 and hand the tray to Josh, then head over to the girls on a bachelorette party. "A cocktail on the house for the bride-to-be?"

The girls point to a brunette, and I hand her the cocktail in a large gin glass which resembles a fish bowl.

"Oooh, thank you."

"Congratulations. I hope you'll be as happy as my wife and I."

She looks up. "You're married?"

"Yep, my kid's due any day now."

"That's lovely. Congratulations to you too."

I head back behind the bar to pour more drinks and pull the lever down to fill a pint of Stella

"Zac," Josh shouts.

I turn my head to see him rush over. "It's happening. Her water's broke, and she's asking for you to get the hospital bag."

My mouth drops. Blood rushes from my head as the room rotates, sending everything into a blurry haze. I take a step forward to steady myself, holding onto the pump. Beer pours down my slacks as the pint overflows, jolting me back to the present. *Fuck. Not again*. I haven't had a spill in ages.

I'm going to be a father. I'm actually going to be a father, and I'm determined to be a damn good one, too.

Enjoyed the book?

Thank you for reading, I hope you enjoyed this story and were able to have a little escape of your own.

Your opinion matters, reviews make an author's world go round!

Please leave me a review on **Amazon**, **Goodreads**, or **Bookbub** and please feel free to share on social media and tag me. I love seeing your posts.

Looking for your next Spicy Rom Com?

If you enjoyed When My Ship Comes In, you'll love

Unwrapped For You

An Enemies to Lovers, Opposites attract novella.

ACKNOWLEDGEMENTS

ıversation with friends sparked an idea. An idea grew
into a story and that story became a book.
want to thank my writer friends for your support,
usiasm, passion, encouragement, skills and planning.

ank you to my Yorkshire Lasses who are always on
l to offer advice, support and a pick-me-up whenever
needed (which has been quite a lot, haha).

ank you to all my beta readers. Your comments and
gestions helped whip this story into shape (and Zac,
ı he wouldn't behave). I am eternally grateful for your
ı and eyes on this. As always, there is a little bit of all
of you in this book.

y ARC readers. Thank you for taking the time to read
l review this book. I love reading your thoughts and
ıg all your amazing edits. Thank you once again from
the bottom of my heart.

last but not least. My family. The hours upon hours it
ɔs to write, re-write, and re-write again is time spent
ıy from my family. Without their unconditional love,
port and understanding it would not be possible for
my stories to be told.

ABOUT THE Author

Annie Charme lives in the heart of England with her
husband, two children and a randy dog.
She is a graphic artist by day and author by night.
When she isn't working, you will find her enjoying time
with her family in the English countryside or curled up on
the sofa with a coffee, blanket, dog and a kissing book.

Being an avid reader of romance novels, Annie feels that
the average woman is not represented enough, and books
about full-figured women are very few and far between.
This is something that sparked her passion for writing.

www.anniecharme.com

ALSO BY ANNIE CHARME

Spicy RomCom

Unwrapped For You

A Curves For Christmas Novella

Hate Tea Love You

A Man of The Month Club Novella

The Temptation Series

Forever Young

A Prequel, The Temptation Series

Forever Yours

Book 1 of The Temptation Series

Forever Mine

Book 2 of The Temptation Series

Romantic Suspense

Protecting Poppy

Novella, out in June 2023

Taming Violet

Out Summer 2023

Made in the USA
Middletown, DE
01 February 2023

23657194R00137